TOOK

A Ghost Story

MARY DOWNING HAHN

CLARION BOOKS
Houghton Mifflin Harcourt
Boston   New York

Clarion Books

215 Park Avenue South,

New York, New York 10003

Clarion Books is an imprint of Houghton Mifflin Harcourt Publishing Company.

www.hmhco.com

The text was set in 14.5 Aged Book Regular and 11.5 Minister Light Std.

Library of Congress Cataloging-in-Publication Data

Hahn, Mary Downing.

Took : a ghost story / Mary Downing Hahn.

pages cm

Summary: "A witch called Old Auntie is lurking near Dan's family's new home.
He doesn't believe in her at first, but is forced to accept that she is real and take
action when his little sister, Erica, is 'took' to become Auntie's slave for the next
fifty years"—Provided by publisher.

ISBN 978-0-544-55153-4 (hardcover)

[1. Witches—Fiction. 2. Horror stories.] I. Title.

PZ7.H1256To 2015

Fic]—dc23

2014043064

Manufactured in the United States of America

DOC 10 9 8 7 6 5 4 3 2 1

4500544000

TOOK

The Beginning

The old woman stands on the hilltop, just on the edge of the woods, well hidden from the farmhouse below. Two men and a woman are getting out of a car that has a sign for Jack Lingo Realty painted on the side. The old woman has seen plenty of Realtors in her time. She doesn't know this one, but she remembers his pa, old Jack Lingo, and *his* pa, Edward, and the one afore him, back and back through the years to the first Lingo ever to settle in this valley and take up the buying and selling of houses.

Though young Lingo doesn't know it, Auntie is helping him sell that house to the man and the woman in the only way she knows – muttering and humming and moving her hands this way and that way, weaving spells in the air, sending messages as she's always done. Messages that make folks need things not worth needing. Dangerous things. Things they regret getting.

You might wonder why Auntie wants this man and woman to buy the house. Truth to tell, she doesn't give a hoot about them. They're ignorant fools, but they have something she wants, and she aims to get it. It's almost time for the change, and they've come on schedule, just as she'd known they would.

"New for old," she chants to herself. "Strong for weak, healthy for sickly, pretty for ugly."

When the man and the woman follow young Lingo into the old Estes house, Auntie sways back and forth, grinning and rubbing her dry, bony hands together. Her skirt blows in the wind, and long strands of white hair whip around her face. With a little hop and a jig, she turns to something hidden in the trees behind her. "Won't be long now, my boy. We'll get rid of the old pet and get us a new one to raise up."

Though he stays out of sight, her companion makes a noise like a hog when it's hungry – a squealing sort of snort that might be a laugh, or it might be something else altogether.

Auntie gazes down at the rundown farmhouse and

outbuildings, the overgrown fields, the woods creeping closer year by year. From the hill, she can see the missing shingles in the roof, the warped boards riddled with termites and dry rot, the cracks in the chimney.

Almost fifty years have passed since the Estes family left the place. Nobody has lived there since then. Local folk avoid the place. They scare their children with stories about the girl, the one before her, and the one before her, back and back to the very first girl. Fear keeps them out of the woods and away from the cabin on Brewster's Hill. Those children know all about Auntie and her companion.

But newcomers always show up, city people who've never heard the stories. If the valley folk try to warn them, they scoff and laugh and call the stories superstitious nonsense. They come from places where lights burn all night. They don't heed the dark and what hides there.

It all works to Auntie's advantage.

Down below, a door opens, and Auntie watches young Lingo lead the man and woman outside. Even though they speak softly, Auntie hears every word. They aim to buy that tumbledown wreck of a house, fix it up, and live there with their children, a boy and a girl, they tell him. It's just what they want – a chance to get away from their old life and start anew in the country. They'll get some chickens, they say, a couple of goats, maybe even a cow or a sheep. They'll plant a garden, grow their own food.

The man and the woman get into the Realtor's car, laughing, excited. Auntie spits into the dirt. Fools. They'll find out soon enough.

She listens to the car's engine until she can't hear it anymore. Then she snaps her fingers and does another jig. "It's falling into place just like I predicted, dear boy, but don't you say a word to her back at the cottage. She ain't to know till it happens."

Her companion snorts and squeals, and the two of them disappear into the dark woods.

To wait.

ONE

It was a long drive from Fairfield, Connecticut, to Woodville, West Virginia— two days, with an overnight stay in Maryland. My sister, Erica, and I were sick of the back seat, sick of each other, and mad at our parents for making us leave our home, our school, and our friends.

Had they asked us how we felt about moving? Of course not. They've never been the kind of parents who ask if you want to drink your milk from the red glass or the blue glass. They just hand you a glass, and that's that. Milk tastes the same whether the glass is blue or red or purple.

Going to West Virginia was a big thing, something we should have had a say in, but no. They left us with a neighbor, drove down there, found a house they liked, and bought it. Just like that.

They were the grownups, the adults, the parents. They were in charge. They made the decisions.

In all fairness, they had a reason for what they did. Dad worked for a big corporation. He earned a big salary. We had a big house, two big cars, and all sorts of other big stuff—expensive stuff. Erica and I went to private school. Mom didn't work. She was what's called a soccer mom, driving me and Erica and our friends to games and clubs and the country club pool. She and Dad played golf. They were planning to buy a sailboat.

But then the recession came along, and the big corporation started laying people off. Dad was one of them. He thought he'd find another job fast, but he didn't. A year went by. One of our big cars was repossessed. Erica and I went to public school. We gave up the country club. There was no more talk about sailboats.

The bank started sending letters. Credit card

compani?s called. Dad and Mom were maxed out financially. The mortgage company threatened foreclosure.

So we had to sell the house. I can understand that. But why did we have to move to West Virginia? It was cheaper to live there, Dad said. Erica and I would love it. So much space—woods and fields and mountains. He took to singing "Country Roads," an old John Denver song about West Virginia, putting lots of emphasis on "Almost heaven, West Virginia." He also informed us that the license plates said "Wild, Wonderful."

So here we were, on an interstate highway, with nothing to see but mountains and woods, wild but not wonderful, in my opinion. It was like being in a foreign country. How would I ever get used to all the nature surrounding us?

Beside me, Erica was talking to the doll Mom had given her—not because it was her birthday or anything, but because she was so unhappy about leaving Fairfield.

That's rewarding bad behavior, if you ask me. I was just as unhappy as my sister, but since I didn't cry myself to sleep and mope in my room and refuse to eat, all I got was a pair of binoculars and Peterson's *Field Guide to Birds of North America*. Dad thought I might like to identify the birds we were sure to see when we went hiking. Well, maybe I would, but still, that doll was ten times more expensive than my binoculars. It came with a little trunk full of clothes. There were even outfits in my sister's size so she and the doll could dress alike. It had its own bed, too. And its hair was red just like Erica's and cut the same way.

All the time we were in the van, Erica talked to the doll. She tried all its clothes on and told the doll how pretty it was. She hugged it and kissed it. She even named it Little Erica.

It was making me sick. But every time I complained, Erica got mad and we started quarreling and Mom turned around and blamed it all on me. "Leave your sister alone, Daniel," she'd say. "She's perfectly happy playing with Little Erica. Read a book or something."

"You know I can't read in the car. Do you want me to barf all over that stupid doll?"

At last we turned off the interstate. The roads narrowed and ran up and down hills, crossed fields, passed farms, and tunneled through woods. We glimpsed mountains and swift rivers. The towns were farther apart and smaller, some no more than a strip of houses and shops along the road.

By the time Dad finally pulled off an unpaved road and headed down a narrow driveway, the woods around us were dark. In the van's headlights the trees looked like a stage set lit by spotlights.

The van bounced over ruts and bumps, tossing Erica and me toward and away from each other. "Stay on your side, Daniel," Erica said, "and stop banging into me and Little Erica. We don't like it."

"That doll doesn't care — she's not real."

"She is so!"

"Be quiet, Daniel," Mom said.

"It's not my fault," I said. "Instead of blaming me, tell Dad to slow down."

Just then we came out of the woods, and I got my first view of the house. It stood in the middle of a field of tall grass — weeds, actually. Even in the dark

I could see that the place was a wreck. The porch sagged under the weight of vines growing up the walls and across the roof. Tall, shaggy bushes blocked most of the windows on the first floor. Shutters hung crooked. Some were missing altogether. I was sure it hadn't been painted for a long time.

Erica was the first to speak. "It's scary."

"What's scary about it?" Dad asked.

"It's dark." She hugged her doll tightly. "The woods are scary, too. And there aren't any other houses."

"Wait until morning, Erica," Mom said. "It's lovely in the daylight. You'll see."

"And we have a few neighbors down the road," Dad added.

How far down the road? I wondered. And what were they like?

Dad and Mom got out of the van and headed toward the house. Erica ran to catch up and slipped her hand into Mom's. I followed them, breathing in the unfamiliar smell of the woods and listening to night sounds. Wind rattled branches and hissed through the weeds in the field. A shutter banged against the side of the house. An owl called from the woods.

At the same moment, something made the hair on my neck rise. Sure that someone was watching us, I turned around and stared down the dark driveway. I saw no one, but I shivered — and not because I was cold.

Arrival

The old woman stands on the hilltop, at the edge of the woods, well hidden from the farmhouse below, just as she did before, but now it's a dark, cold night, lit by the moon. All around her, bushes and branches rattle in a wind that carries autumn's breath. But she isn't cold. She leans on her staff and peers toward the road.

"They're coming," she calls to her companion. He snorts and continues snuffling about in the dead leaves for good things to eat.

Headlights bounce down the driveway. A big car stops by the house. Even in the dark a person can see that it's a ramshackle wreck of a place, ready to topple with the first strong wind that comes its way.

The car doors open and the interior lights come on. She sees the girl, just the one she needs. The child gets out, clutching a dolly. The old woman sniffs fear. The girl is scared of the dark and the old house. She doesn't want to live here. Well, she won't live here long, will she?

The girl's name is blown by the wind across the dark field and laid at the old woman's feet. Erica. Air-ric-cah. She likes to draw the name out, especially the last syllable.

"Air-ric-cah, Air-ric-cah," the old woman whispers. The name glides lightly through the air, a rustle of black silk thread, and winds itself into the girl's ear.

She sees the girl tense and look around, move closer to her mother.

"Yes," the old woman hisses. "You'll do. Air-ric-cah, Air-ric-cah."

She does one of her little jigs and calls to her companion. "Time to go, dear boy. We'll see her soon, don't you worry. She's the one, she's ours."

As the family enters their new home, the old woman and her companion wrap themselves in darkness and make their way home.

TWO

While we waited on the porch, Dad fished a big old-fashioned key out of his pocket. With a lot of effort he finally got it to turn in the lock. Moonlight followed us inside and cast our shadows across the dusty floor. In front of us, stairs led to the second story.

Mom flicked a switch, and the shadows fled. To the right was the living room, or maybe the parlor, empty now except for a fireplace. Three tall windows with old-fashioned wavy glass reflected us standing in the hall, slightly distorted, like people in a fun house.

"Where's our furniture?" Erica asked.

"It's coming tomorrow," Mom told her.

"But where are we sleeping?" she asked, sounding a bit tearful.

"Don't you remember?" Dad asked. "We brought our camping stuff—sleeping bags, foam mats, pillows, blankets."

"Can I sleep with Mommy?"

"Of course you can." Mom put her arm around Erica and hugged her.

I was getting pretty tired of Erica's clinging behavior. "What's wrong with you?" I whispered. "You never used to act like this."

"I never had to live in the woods before." She turned to Mom. "Are we going to eat wild berries?"

"Of course not, sweetie," Dad said. "Whatever gave you that idea?"

"That's what happens sometimes in stories."

"Well, this isn't a story, Erica," Mom said.

Dad got an ancient gas stove going, and Mom heated a pot of water. When it boiled, she dumped in noodles and heated a jar of marinara sauce.

We ate our first meal in the house picnic style in front of the fire. Erica snuggled beside Mom and shared her food with Little Erica. The food stuck to the doll's face, and Erica tenderly wiped her clean with a napkin.

Later, we all crawled into our sleeping bags and watched what was left of the fire fall into ash. The lights were out, and the moon shone in through the tall windows. I heard Erica whispering to the doll.

Sometime during the night I woke up. I'd drunk too much soda at dinner, and now I needed the bathroom. I eased out of my sleeping bag and got to my feet. Dad snored, Mom slept like a dead woman, and Erica murmured as if she were dreaming.

I tiptoed across the floor and eased the front door open. It was easier to pee outside than find my way upstairs to the bathroom.

The moonlight was brilliant and the stars were clustered thickly over my head, more than I'd ever seen in Fairfield. After I finished what I came out to do, I stood on the porch and gazed at the dark mass of woods bordering the fields. The night was cold, but as I turned to go inside, I was stopped by a sound in the darkness—a howl, which might have been the wind in the trees but was scarier. Much scarier. I shivered and edged toward the door, but before I stepped inside, I looked back. Something moved at the edge of the woods. Its head gleamed in the moonlight, as white as bone. I heard the howl again, louder this time, and stumbled backward, slamming and bolting the door.

"Daniel," Mom called sleepily, "what are you doing up in the middle of the night?"

"I went outside to pee. Something in the woods howled." I slid into my sleeping bag, shivering with cold and fear.

"Shh," she whispered. "You'll wake up Dad and Erica."

"Didn't you hear it?"

She shook her head. "It was probably an owl or a fox."

"No. I saw it," I told her. "It was as tall as a man, and its head shone in the moonlight."

Mom smoothed my hair. "Go back to sleep, Daniel. There's nothing out there. It's dark, you're in a strange place, and your eyes were playing tricks on you."

I moved a little closer to her. Maybe she was right. She must be right. Monsters didn't roam the woods anywhere but in fairy tales. I closed my eyes and practiced breathing slowly and deeply, but it was almost daylight by the time I fell asleep.

When I woke up, sunlight filled the living room. Just as Mom had said, whatever I'd heard and seen in the dark had a natural explanation—night noises most likely, animals going about their nocturnal business, embellished with my imagination. Moonlight and shadows play tricks on you.

The moving truck arrived before we'd finished breakfast, and Mom put us all to work. We picked our bedrooms first. Mine overlooked the woods, which were not quite as close to the house as I'd thought the night before, but close enough for me to see a deer pause at the edge of the trees and then vanish into the shadows. The lawns in Connecticut were overrun with deer, but this was a wild deer and therefore more noble than the ones who ate our shrubbery and our flowers and the vegetables Mom tried to grow.

Erica's room was across the hall from mine, at the front of the house. Mom and Dad were next to her. The bedroom beside mine was reserved for Dad—his office, he called it. At the end of the hall was a small room, probably a sewing room, Mom said, or a nursery. She claimed it for her weaving. "The loom will fit just right under the windows," she said.

The moving men spent most of the day tramping around the house, upstairs and down, putting furniture where Mom told them to. When they finally drove away, Mom gave us our next tasks. Unpack our clothes and belongings and put them away.

I finished first and stopped in Erica's room to see how she was doing. Her clothes lay in a heap on her unmade bed. Her boxes of toys and books sat in the middle of the floor, where the moving men had left them, still taped shut. Erica sat on a window seat, her back to me. She held Little Erica.

"We don't like it here," Erica whispered to the doll. "It's a bad, scary place, no matter what they say. You and I know, but nobody believes us."

Little Erica had nothing to say that I could hear, but my sister bent her head close to the doll as if she were listening to her. "Yes," she murmured. "Yes."

I hated to interrupt the weird conversation, but I stepped into the room and said, "Mom told you to put your stuff away, but you haven't even started."

Erica whirled around. Her red hair swung like

a flag. And so did the doll's. "I'm never going to put anything away until we go home."

"*This* is home now." I picked up a box labeled SOCKS AND UNDERWEAR and pried off the tape. "I'll help you."

"Leave my things alone!" Erica laid the doll down and snatched the box away. "Get out of my room, Daniel. We don't want you here."

"What's going on?" Mom stood in the doorway.

"I was just trying to help her unpack."

"I don't want him to help," Erica said. "I'm leaving everything just like this until we go home."

"Honey, we *are* home." Mom tried to hug her, but she pulled away.

"Home is Connecticut," Erica whispered. "Not *here*."

Mom made a gesture toward the door. "Leave this to me, Daniel."

As I left the room, Mom shut the door. I lingered in the hall for a moment. Mom was talking softly. Erica was crying.

I found Dad in the basement in front of a huge furnace that looked like something you'd find on the

Nautilus, all dials and levers and doors and pipes. A submarine engine only Captain Nemo understood. Steampunk in every way.

"Let me see," Dad mused. "It's September. Hopefully, I'll have time to figure out how this monster works before we need it."

I pictured a long, cold winter, with the four of us huddled around the fireplace to keep warm.

"Or maybe I can call somebody from the oil company," Dad went on, "and he can explain it to me."

We stood side by side and looked around the basement. It was dark and dank and musty. The ceiling was so low Dad could barely stand up straight. Pipes festooned with cobwcbs hung even lower. The only light was a bare bulb hanging by a cord from a crossbeam. The floor was dirt, the walls stone. The damp air smelled as if it had been trapped down here since the house was built.

"Once I establish myself as a photographer," Dad said, "we'll fix this basement up. Replace the furnace with something new that I can understand. Put in some windows, maybe a sliding glass door. I could even build a darkroom and get out my old film cameras."

While Dad was picturing a darkroom and sliding glass doors, I was imagining a murderer carrying his victims down the steep, rickety steps and digging graves in the dirt floor.

"I'm going outside," I told Dad. "I could use some fresh air."

Leaving him poking around in the junk piled in every corner, I found Mom at the kitchen table, busy sorting napkins and tablecloths. Erica was sitting near her, reading *Bedtime for Frances* to Little Erica. Neither of them noticed me, so I slipped out the back door to do some exploring.

The house looked even worse in daylight. Peeling paint exposed bare gray wood. A gutter dangled from the eaves, and a downspout lay in the weeds. Judging by the number of shingles I saw on the ground, the roof probably leaked. The porch floorboards were warped, the railing was loose, and the steps tilted to one side.

Behind the house, I discovered a small tumbledown barn almost hidden under a tangle of wild grapevines, honeysuckle, poison ivy, and brambles. All around it grew a jungle of pokeberry weeds taller than I was. Poisonous berries hung from the red stalks in black clusters, like grapes. Sticking up from the weeds were two doorless refrigerators, an old plow, an ancient Ford pickup truck, several rusted air conditioners, and a mildewed sofa. The town dump, I thought, right in our own backyard.

What were Dad and Mom thinking when they bought this place? Had they lost their minds? We'd never get the house fixed up, let alone clear the junk out. I felt like packing my belongings and siding with Erica. Maybe between the two of us we could persuade Mom and Dad to go back to Connecticut.

THREE

The next day, we went to Home Depot. We couldn't afford to paint the outside of the house yet. That would have to wait. But we could afford to make the inside look better.

I chose blue for my room, and Erica chose lavender for hers. Mom and Dad picked shades of beige for everything else, except for the kitchen, which was to be yellow. A bright, cheerful color, Mom said.

It took a week to paint the house. All of us, even Erica, helped scrape and sand and clean the walls. When we finally finished, the place looked more like home—our pictures on the walls, our furniture in the rooms, our books on the shelves. We ate dinner at our dining room table using our plates and glasses and silverware. We ate breakfast and lunch at our kitchen table. Mom's collection of teapots appeared on a shelf in a kitchen. Dad helped her set up a loom in the little room upstairs. He organized his office and arranged his pipe collection in his barrister bookcase. He hung his diploma from UMass.

In my room, I lined up my books on a shelf Dad made for me. I kept my Star Wars figures and my puzzle collection on their own shelves. Posters of Spider-Man and Captain America hung on one wall. A movie ad for *The Hobbit* hung between the windows on the opposite wall. I was beginning to feel at home.

Erica finally unpacked her boxes and hung up her clothes. She folded underwear and socks and T-shirts and put them in bureau drawers. She arranged books and found places for her dolls and stuffed animals.

When she was finished, her room looked exactly like her room in Fairfield—her lavender checked curtains fit the new windows and the paint matched her old walls. The only difference was the view—woods and fields and mountains instead of green lawns and neighbors' houses.

The next week, Mom enrolled Erica and me in school. It was our first trip to Woodville itself. The shopping center on the outskirts of town had a Home Depot, a Walmart, and a Piggly Wiggly grocery store, as well as a nail salon, a liquor store, an insurance agent, a bank, Joe's Pizza, and a real estate office with faded photos of houses for sale taped to the windows. What more did we need, Dad asked.

Whatever it was, we wouldn't find it in Woodville. Except for a used-clothing store, a bar, and a thrift shop, the buildings on Main Street were boarded up. Even the graffiti was faded.

Narrow streets ran uphill from one side of Main Street and downhill from the other side. Dogs barked as we drove by. A gust of wind blew newspapers down the street. We didn't see a single person. The whole town could have been abandoned, as far as I could tell. Except for the dogs, of course.

"Next time we'll take the scenic route," Mom said, "if there is one."

She turned off Main Street and drove uphill through a neighborhood of old houses that were slightly nicer than the ones we'd seen so far. The Woodville School was at the top of the hill—kindergarten through eighth grade, which meant that Erica's second grade classroom and my seventh grade classroom would be in the same building. The school was made of dark gray stone and had tall, narrow windows; a steep flight of steps led to the main entrance, a big black door. It might as well have been named the Bastille School for bad boys and girls.

Erica clung to Mom's hand. "I don't want to go here. It's ugly."

"Don't be silly." Shaking her hand free, Mom pulled open the door. "It will be fine," she added. "Just give it time."

I knew by the uncertainty in her voice that she didn't believe her own words. But what could she do? It was the only school in town.

Mom led us into an office filled with old-fashioned dark furniture. A thin woman looked up from a typewriter and did a funny thing with her mouth, which I think was meant to be a smile. Her hair was pulled tightly back from her face, and she wore a plain black dress with long sleeves. She scared Erica and made me nervous. Even Mom looked uncomfortable. According to the sign on her desk, she was Miss Danvers, school secretary.

"You must be Mrs. Anderson," she said to Mom. "And you are Erica and Daniel, if I'm not mistaken. Welcome to Woodville Elementary."

While Erica and I sat side by side, as silent as mutes, Mom filled out forms. Miss Danvers returned to her typing. I watched, fascinated by the sight of a real live person using an antique instead of a computer.

"Their official transcripts should arrive any day," Mom said as she handed Miss Danvers the completed paperwork.

A bald man with a gray mustache stuck his head out of an inner door and smiled at us. "I'm Mr. Sykes, the principal. I hope you two will enjoy our school— a bit smaller than you're used to, I'm sure. Not as up to date, maybe, but—" The phone in his office rang, and he excused himself to answer it.

I knew sarcasm when I heard it.

Miss Danvers led the three of us down a hall. The walls were grayish green and bare. No bright paintings, no starred reports, no posters. The closed doors to classrooms were unadorned too. It was very different from the schools I'd gone to in Connecticut.

Miss Danvers stopped at a door labeled SEVENTH GRADE. "Wait here," she told Mom and Erica.

Opening the door, she ushered me into the room. The teacher was a large woman with a stern face. She looked at me as if I were an invasive species.

The kids in the room stared at me. They sat in old-fashioned one-piece desks arranged in straight rows from the front to the back of the room. No artwork. No projects. Just the flag and a faded portrait of George Washington. The blackboard was made of slate, and sticks of chalk and erasers lay on the ledge beneath it. It looked like a classroom from an old black-and-white movie.

I glanced over my shoulder. Mom was staring into the room in disbelief. "Daniel, this is Miss Mincham, your teacher," Miss Danvers said. Turning to the class, she added, "Boys and girls, Daniel's from Connecticut, that little state near New York City."

Their eyes flicked over me, taking in my khaki pants, turtleneck sweater, and parka—standard clothing in either Pine Ridge or Carson Middle

School, but not here. The uniform for both boys and girls seemed to be jeans and T-shirts, old and faded and either too big or too small.

A boy in the back of the room snickered. He must have been fifteen or sixteen years old, from the size of him. Two girls whispered to each other and giggled.

Miss Mincham rose to her feet, an awe-inspiring sight. Almost six feet tall and weighing about two hundred pounds, she frowned at the boy in the back row and the two girls. Then she told me to take a seat in the back row—the empty one next to the giant boy.

The class was studying history. Miss Mincham called out events from the Revolutionary War and asked kids to supply the dates when they happened. I've never been good at remembering stuff like that, so I didn't do any better than the rest of them. When she shifted the subject to math, she sent us to the blackboard for drills in long division. English consisted of reciting rules of grammar. And geography was naming capitals of foreign countries.

In the cafeteria, a kid knocked my lunch tray out of my hand and pretended it was an accident. In gym class, a bunch of boys cornered me in the locker room and shoved me around, sneering at my clothes and my snobby accent. Ignoring their behavior, the gym teacher blew his whistle and yelled, "Okay, that's enough, out on the floor, let's play some basketball." I was bumped into, tripped, and hit on the head with the ball—all accidentally of course.

By the end of the day, I hated Woodville School. I found Erica, and we boarded the bus that would take us home. The driver was a woman named Mrs. Plummer, the first nice person I'd met all day. She told us our stop was the last one. "It's a long ride," she said.

As we rumbled along narrow roads, uphill and down, letting kids off at farms and trailer parks along the way, the boy behind me kicked the back of my seat, and his friend said things like "I'm from Connecticut and I'm better than you," in what he thought was a good imitation of the accent I never knew I had.

Finally, there was only one kid on the bus beside Erica and me. Despite the lurching ride, he staggered up the aisle and sat down in front of us. Leaning over the back of the seat, he stared at us. He was maybe ten years old, a scrawny boy with dingy blond hair and sad brown eyes. He looked as if soap was not used in his house, either on him or on his clothes.

"My stop is the last one," he said. "Did you forget to get off?"

"No," I said. "We're the last stop."

He shook his head. "There's no stop after mine."

"We just moved here," I told him. "We live on a farm, just over the bridge."

His eyes widened. "You live on the Estes family farm?"

I shrugged. "Maybe. I don't know who used to live in our house."

I glanced at Erica, who was staring at the boy.

"Is something wrong with where we live?" she asked.

"It's where the girl disappeared," he said.

"What girl?"

I nudged her. "Don't listen to him. He's just trying to scare us."

He looked at me. "I'm not lying, if that's what you think. Just ask anybody about Selene Estes. They'll tell you." He shoved his face close to Erica's.

"Something got her and drug her away and nobody ever saw her again."

Erica drew back, her eyes fearful.

"Nothing dragged her away," I told him. "She got lost and fell off a cliff or something."

"Hah," the boy said. "That's what you think. There's things out in these woods people from Conneck-ti-cut ain't never heard of."

With a grinding of gears, the bus stopped and the boy got off. I looked out the window and saw him standing by the road, making a face at me. Then we jolted and bumped and swayed around a curve and up a hill, leaving him and his stories behind.

The bus made its next and final stop at the end of our driveway. As we got off, the driver, Mrs. Plummer, leaned out the door and called, "Don't believe anything Brody Mason tells you. He's a born liar, that boy."

As the bus drove away, Erica turned to me. "Do you think a girl disappeared from our house?"

"Of course not," I said. "You heard what the bus driver said. Brody or Brady, or whatever his name is, is a liar. He was trying to scare you."

"He did scare me." She fumbled to adjust the shoulder strap on her backpack. "He wasn't lying, Daniel, I could tell."

I straightened her strap for her. "Listen, Erica, that boy was definitely lying. And do you know why? The kids here don't like us. We're outsiders. That's why they're so mean."

Erica turned to me, her eyes bright with tears. "My teacher, Mrs. Kline, is mean, too, even meaner than Miss Davis back at public school in Fairfield. She kept me in at recess and made me write one hundred times 'I will not daydream in class.' The girl who sits behind me whispered that I'm ugly. At lunchtime, all the girls laughed at me and said I talk funny and wear weird clothes. They wouldn't let me sit at a table with them either."

"It was exactly the same in my class," I told her. "I got beaten up in gym, and my teacher called me stupid because I didn't know the capital of Rhodesia or the exact date George Washington crossed the Delaware, let alone rules of grammar, which nobody ever taught me."

"Maybe Mom will teach us at home."

I shook my head. "No. She'll just tell us to be

patient and the kids will start liking us. You know, all of a sudden they'll realize how nice we are. Even if we do come from Connecticut."

"You don't believe that, do you?"

"No," I said. "In fact, I don't think even Mom believes it."

Erica frowned. "Do you hear noises at night?"

I looked at her, surprised by the sudden change of subject. "Do you?"

"Sometimes I hear a sort of whispering. Almost like somebody's calling me. It sounds like this—*Air-ric-cah, Air-ric-cah*."

She said it in a low, scary voice—a weird, drawn-out version of her name.

"It's just the wind," I told her. "Hear it blowing in the tops of the trees? It sounds like it's whispering up there."

Erica shook her head. "No, it's not like trees or wind. It's my name. Then it whispers other things. I can almost make out the words, but not quite."

She broke away from me then and ran to meet Mom on the front porch, her red hair flying in the breeze, her backpack bouncing.

I followed her slowly, thinking about what she'd

said. I was sure that Erica had imagined the whispering voice, but when I looked at the woods behind the
house, I felt my chest tighten with anxiety. In the late-
afternoon light, the shadows of the trees stretched
across the field. The woods were already dark, and
the mountainsides were in shadow.

Mom waved to me from the porch, and I broke
into a run, suddenly eager to be inside, safe from
whatever might be hiding in those woods—things
that didn't exist in Connecticut.

FOUR

After dinner that night, Erica told Mom and Dad about the boy on the bus and what he'd told us. Our parents agreed with me. This was an old, old farm, and no one had lived in the house for a long time. It was exactly the sort of place that inspired people to make up stories.

"It must be a country version of an urban legend," Dad said. "Like the man with the—"

Mom stopped him with a sharp look.

"The man with a what?" Erica asked.

"The man with a monkey," I said, to rescue Dad. I definitely didn't want him telling Erica about the man with the hook. In fact, I myself didn't want to hear that story, not here, not at night, not when anything could be out there howling in the dark, watching us through the tall living room windows Mom hadn't gotten around to covering with curtains.

"Does the monkey disappear?" Erica persisted.

"Of course not," I told her. "He and the man run away from the circus and live happily ever after in a tarpaper shack."

Erica laughed. "And they eat wild berries for breakfast, lunch, and dinner?"

Dad winked at me. "Exactly!"

Erica snuggled beside Mom on the couch and listened to a chapter of *The Moffats,* a book Mom loved when she was Erica's age. And still did.

But when it was time for bed, Erica said, "I don't want to go upstairs. It's so dark outside my window."

"Daniel's right across the hall from you," Mom said, "and Dad and I are in the next room."

"Will you come with me, Mommy?" Erica asked. "And tuck me in and sit with me till I fall asleep?"

Dad sighed. "Give in now, Martha, and it'll be the same every night."

Either Mom didn't hear him, or she ignored him.

Scooping Erica up as if she were still a baby, she carried her upstairs.

Dad shook his head. "Your mother is spoiling that child."

I shrugged, opened my odious social studies book, and began memorizing the imports, exports, and native products of Germany. What a waste of time Woodville School was. My textbook had been published thirty years ago.

When I passed Erica's door later, I heard my sister say, "Are you sure it's just a legend?"

"Yes," Mom said. "Please stop worrying about it. No one disappeared. A girl named Selene never lived here. That boy was a liar."

The next morning, Erica and I sat in the front of the school bus, right behind Mrs. Plummer. The bus slowed for the second stop, and Brody got on. Erica stared out the window, pretending not to see him, but I gave him a dirty look. He made an ugly face, sat down behind us, and began kicking the back of my seat.

As the bus filled with kids, Brody told them where Erica and I lived.

One girl said she never walked down the road past our driveway. Her friend claimed that her big sister and some of her friends drove up the driveway on a dare. It was few years ago, when no one lived in the house.

"They heard people crying and wailing and calling Selene's name. They didn't see nothing, but they got out of there fast."

Erica pressed her fingers in her ears and hummed, but I listened to every word. If I was dumb enough to believe their stories, a family named Estes lived on the farm about forty or fifty years ago, maybe more, no one was sure. It was before they were born, but their parents or maybe their grandparents remembered it. They had a daughter named Selene, and she disappeared when she was seven years old, and no one ever found her. One girl said she was *took*. Maybe it was the demons in the woods, a boy suggested. Maybe Old Auntie the conjure woman up on Brewster's Hill got her, Brody said. Or, worst of all, a girl said, Old Auntie's razorback hog, the one called Bloody Bones, ate her up.

Nobody agreed about who took Selene, but they all agreed she was never found.

By the time we arrived at school, Erica was trembling. We waited until the bus was empty and then got up to leave.

Mrs. Plummer stopped Erica. "Don't let them scare you," she told my sister. "It's just a yarn people been spinning for years, not a speck of truth in it. A girl named Selene disappeared, but she wasn't 'took.' There's no conjure woman and no Bloody Bones."

She rummaged in her purse, pulled out a pack of Life Savers, and handed it to Erica. "Help yourself. You, too."

We each took one and thanked her. "They're not really bad kids," Miss Plummer said. "Just nobody's taught them manners. They've grown up as wild as bears in the woods. Give them time. They'll get friendly when they're used to you."

A week passed, and another week followed, but those kids didn't get used to Erica and me. They didn't even try. Luckily, Mrs. Plummer saved the seat behind her for us, so no one could say or do anything to us without getting kicked off the bus.

Even so, they found ways to torment us with stories of Selene Estes. A whisper here, a comment there, a note or a drawing passed to us.

When we were off the bus, with no Mrs. Plummer to protect us, the boys continued to knock me around on the playground and the girls whispered about Erica. Unlike Mrs. Plummer, our teachers never noticed. Or maybe they just didn't care.

Mom and Dad didn't have any more luck in Woodville than we did—the adults disliked them for the same reasons the kids disliked Erica and me. They were especially offended by our failure to join the only church in town. We weren't only outsiders, we were godless outsiders.

As far as jobs went, neither Dad nor Mom found a position in Woodville. Not that there was much to choose from.

Dad finally got a job at Home Depot, where he wore a big orange apron and helped people find tools, paint, garbage cans, plumbing supplies, and whatever else they were looking for, most often the restrooms.

Soon after, Mom landed a position as a receptionist at the real estate office on the other side of the parking lot from Home Depot. Nobody there cared where my parents came from or if they went to church. The people who worked at the shopping center were practically all outsiders themselves, from cities such as Charleston. In Woodville, they claimed, you'd never be accepted if you weren't married to your cousin. Dad laughed at this, but Mom said it was an ignorant way to talk.

On weekends Dad and I got into the habit of spending our free time roaming the woods and fields, following trails made long ago by trappers and hunters. He was forever stopping to take a picture of a lichen-covered boulder or a mossy log, a tangle of branches, a gnarled tree, a hawk or a crow in flight, but I didn't mind. I loved being in the woods with him.

Neither Mom nor Erica went with us. Mom had too much to do, she said, and Erica had no interest in the great outdoors. While Mom busied herself weaving, Erica sat nearby, re-reading the Little House on the Prairie books or playing with Little Erica. Sometimes she drew picture stories in her sketchpads; sometimes she painted with watercolors. She seemed perfectly content until the day ended. When night came, she grew fearful and clung to Mom. She still spoke of hearing scary whispers in the dark corners of her room.

On this particular day, a Saturday, Mom was

working at the Realtor's office. Erica didn't want to stay at home alone, so she agreed to go with Dad and me. Although it was sunny, the wind was brisk, so we pulled on heavy sweaters and wrapped scarves around our necks. Erica dressed Little Erica in a sweater that matched hers and wrapped a bandanna around the doll's neck.

The wind ripped leaves from the trees and filled the air with whirling gold. Dad tried to capture the last of the foliage, but the color had peaked and many of the trees were bare.

His camera swinging from its strap, his hiking stick in hand, Dad chose a trail that led uphill, winding around boulders and outcrops of trees. After a while we came to a steep drop-off on one side of the trail, not exactly a cliff, but high enough to do serious harm, maybe even kill you, if you fell. Just looking down, down, down at the rocks far below was enough to make me step back toward the safe side of the trail, far from the edge.

Erica froze and clung to Dad's hand. "I'm scared of high places," she whispered. "Can we turn around and go home now?"

Leaving Dad to convince Erica that he wouldn't

let her fall, I ran ahead, bounding from rock to rock. If I'd been looking where I was going, I might not have tripped on a tangle of roots half hidden in the fallen leaves, but the next thing I knew, I was flat on the ground on my belly. Struggling to get my breath, I looked through the weeds at a chimney pointing like a finger at the sky.

Scrambling to my feet, I followed an overgrown path to the ruins of an old log cabin that was slowly sinking into the earth. Overgrown with dying vines, shielded by brambles, its walls tilted and sagged. Part of the roof had collapsed under the weight of a fallen tree, but the stone chimney was straight and true.

"Dad, Erica!" I yelled. "There's an old cabin here!"

They made their way through the weeds and undergrowth, Dad leading and Erica following, clutching her doll as if she might be in danger.

We walked around the cabin. Dad took dozens of pictures from every possible angle. He even got down on his stomach to get a different perspective.

"Can we go inside?" I asked.

"I don't see why not." Laughing, Dad knocked at the door. "Just in case."

When he pushed the door open, a buzzard flew out. Dad and I leaped out of its way, and Erica screamed.

"It's just a big bird," Dad told her. "A black buzzard. Nothing to be scared of."

The buzzard landed on a limb and hunched there, staring at us in disapproval. Suddenly he lifted his wings and took off, vanishing into the sky like a streak of black feathers shot from a bow.

"Quoth the buzzard, 'Nevermore,'" Dad said.

Erica looked worried. "Can we go home now?"

"Don't you want to go inside?" Dad asked.

"No." She peered into the darkness beyond the door. "Somebody might be hiding in there."

"Oh, come on." Dad took her hand and led her through the doorway, which was so low he had to stoop to go through it, and I followed close behind.

A little daylight filtered through the vines covering the windows, layers and layers of them twisted together like tangled ropes. The dirt floor reeked of mold. The air smelled of rot and decay and old ashes. I shivered in the damp cold. Suddenly I wanted to go back outside where the sun shone and the air was fresh.

"It smells bad in here," Erica whispered. "Please, Daddy, can we go home?"

"Let's explore first," Dad said. "You never know what you might find in an old place like this."

Although I would never have admitted it, I didn't want to be inside the cabin any more than Erica did. Cobwebs hung like curtains from the rafters; things scuttled in the shadows — mice, insects, I guessed. Weird funguses grew in the dampness. What if we dislodged something and the rest of the roof caved in? We'd be buried alive.

While Erica waited in the doorway, I took a few steps into the cabin. Dad unearthed old bottles, broken pottery, chipped plates and cups — artifacts, he said, to take home and photograph. He was particularly pleased to come across the skulls and bones of several small animals — foxes, raccoons, squirrels, he guessed, that had sheltered and died there.

The little bones were too much for Erica. She retreated to a low stone wall on the edge of the woods and sat in the sun, her head close to her doll's head, having one of her imaginary conversations.

I didn't like the bones any more than my sister did. I didn't like the moldy smell or the damp cold either. In fact, I didn't like anything about the cabin, and I wished Dad would finish taking pictures and get out of there.

"I'm going outside," I told him, "to keep Erica company."

"Okay. I'll be done in here soon, just a few more minutes." With his back turned, he busied himself poking around in a broken-down cupboard, going through things that once belonged to a long-gone stranger.

I sat beside Erica on the wall, glad for the sun on my back and the smell of autumn leaves.

"I want to go home," she said.

"Me, too."

"I wish his camera battery would die."

"Yeah. How many pictures can he take, anyway? There's nothing in there but trash and broken stuff."

"And bones." Erica swung her legs harder, banging her heels. "I don't like bones."

While she smoothed Little Erica's hair, I watched a fuzzy brown caterpillar crawl slowly over the stones. He had a wide black stripe across his back, and I tried to remember if that meant a cold winter was coming.

The longer I sat on the wall, the more I noticed

rustling noises in the woods behind us. An animal, I told myself, moving around in the fallen leaves and underbrush. I turned and peered into the trees, but saw nothing. My neck itched. Someone was there. Maybe Brody and his friends had followed us.

Erica moved closer to me. "Do you hear it now?" she asked.

"Hear what?"

"The whispering." She dropped her voice so low I could barely hear her. "Air-ric-cah, Air-ric-cah—it's calling me. Who is it? What does it want?"

Despite the sun, I felt as if a shadow had passed over us. Even though I couldn't hear the whisper, I sensed that something was behind us in the woods, hidden, watching us. If I told Erica that, she'd be even more scared, so I said, "Nothing's calling you, Erica. You're imagining it."

"You must be deaf." Erica turned away from me and hugged the doll.

At last Dad came out of the cabin. Erica and I waited silently while he prowled around, taking pictures of anything and everything that stayed still long enough—glassless windows, splintered boards, the dark doorway, the chimney, tall weeds, tangles of thorns. He even lined up the things he'd found inside and took pictures of them arranged like still lifes on the wall. A little skull, a cracked plate, a few dead leaves, gloomy stuff.

Finally Dad said, "Come on, let's go." You'd think Erica and I, not him, were the ones who'd wanted to stay. He waved at his collection of junk. "We'll come back later with a bag and get this stuff."

Frankly, I hoped Dad would forget about coming back. I didn't want those things in our house. They'd belonged to someone once. Someone most likely dead by now. The past clung to them like a stain you couldn't wash away.

We headed down the trail toward home, with Erica and me just ahead of Dad. We went slowly, cautiously, watching our step on the steep trail. Sometimes it's harder to go down a hill than to climb it.

Dinner did not go well that night. Mom was upset about her job. Receptionist, ha. A glorified typist, that's all she was. Her boss was stupid and bigoted. He treated her like a servant—do this, do that, fix the coffee, go to Piggly Wiggly, pick up some pastries.

"Oh, you think that's bad," Dad muttered. "Try moving crates of stuff around a store the size of

Home Depot and some manager with a high school education tells you you're doing it wrong. Me doing it wrong. *Me* with an M.B.A. You think I like working there, wearing that big orange apron?"

I ignored them and tried to choke down the stew Mom had spent the afternoon cooking. When I complained that the meat was tough, Dad snapped that tough meat was all we could afford.

"It's got fat in it," Erica said.

"Well, then don't eat it." Dad pushed his chair back and left the table.

"Where are you going, Ted?" Mom asked. "You haven't finished your dinner."

"I'm an adult," Dad said. "I don't need permission to leave the table."

We sat in silence and listened to him climb the stairs. The door to his den closed. He'd spend the rest of the night in there, photoshopping his pictures.

Mom stared at his unfinished dinner. Erica hugged her doll and gazed into space. No one said anything. The shadows of the old house gathered around us.

FIVE

Dad spent more and more time staring at his computer instead of working on his photography. Mom sat in front of her loom and watched the bare trees sway in the wind, but she didn't touch the rug she'd begun weeks earlier. She drank coffee and smoked, an old habit she'd gone back to. It calmed her nerves, she claimed.

She played Joan Baez albums and sang along with sad ballads about death and sorrow. She knew all the words.

Worst of all, she lost interest in cooking. Ever since the night Erica and I complained about the stew meat, she'd begun buying canned soup and canned stew and frozen dinners that she cooked in the microwave. We ate grilled cheese sandwiches at least three nights a week.

Once in a while she came home with a rotisserie chicken from Piggly Wiggly or a pizza from Joe's. As if that were a treat. Back in Fairfield, we went out for pizza at gourmet places. We'd never have eaten one of Joe's pizzas, full of salt and fat and topped off with runny sauce and rubbery cheese.

Nobody said anything about the food. Nobody, not even Erica, complained. We sat at the table and ate what was on our plates. Our conversation consisted of requests for salt or pepper.

Dad worried about money and the leaking roof and dripping faucets. When he wasn't at Home Depot, he wandered around the house making lists of repairs, but instead of doing them, he played games on his computer, something he'd always said was a waste of time.

Erica roamed the house with Little Erica. When I tried to talk to her, she had nothing to say. Every question produced an "I don't know" or a shrug of her shoulders.

Her conversations with the doll grew longer and more frequent. It made me both sad and angry to watch her living this strange imaginary existence. Sad because she used to be a happy, normal kid with real friends. Mad because she persisted in isolating herself from the family, which caused problems between Mom and Dad.

One day, before our parents came home from work, Erica and I were alone in the living room, trapped inside by a cold November rain. As usual, my sister was whispering to Little Erica. I slid closer to hear what she was saying, but she stopped talking and frowned at me as if I'd interrupted a private moment.

I was in a bad mood. I'd flunked another geography test. Someone left a sheet of notebook paper taped to my locker: *"Selene is gonna getcha."* A boy named Caleb Rice tripped me in the hall and got a big laugh out of the kids who saw me take a tumble and drop all my books.

"That doll can't hear a thing you say," I said crossly.

"What do you know about dolls?"

"What everybody knows—everybody but you. They aren't alive."

"Think what you want." Erica smiled as if she knew things I didn't.

"Tell me one thing she can do that a real person does."

"She listens to me. Nobody else does. She talks to me, too. Nobody else does that either."

"Prove it," I said. "Make her say something."

"Little Erica only talks to me."

"You're such a liar." Disgusted with her and myself, I looked out the window. The van was coming down the driveway, its headlights slicing through the dark. "Mom and Dad are here."

Erica shrugged and started combing Little Erica's hair. "I wish I had a sister like *you* instead of a brother like Daniel." She spoke to the doll just loudly enough for me to hear.

The back door opened, and Mom and Dad came in, bringing the cold evening air with them. From the way they acted, neither speaking to nor looking at each other, I knew they'd been quarreling.

Back in the good old Connecticut days, they

hardly ever argued, but now it happened so often they barely spoke to each other without one making the other angry. Usually it was the house. The leak in the roof had gotten worse, and we had to set buckets out to catch the rain. Cold drafts sneaked in through every crack. Dad had figured out the furnace, but the house was never warm. Mom said we lived in a barn.

They were too busy arguing to pay much attention to either Erica or me. I don't think they realized how miserable we were. Or how much they'd changed.

At dinner that night, I said, "Maybe we should go back to Connecticut. Not Fairfield but someplace cheaper, like Bridgeport."

"Bridgeport?" Mom put down her fork and stared at me. "Do you really think we'd be happier in *Bridgeport?*"

"I don't know." I looked at her. "But the schools might be better."

"Doubtful," Dad said.

"They have Home Depots there," I said. "Lowe's, too."

"Oh, that's an inducement," Dad said. "I could

wear my nifty orange apron and show investment bankers where the restrooms are."

"Never mind." I left the table, only to hear raised voices behind me. Erica slunk past me and went to her room.

The days passed, rushing us toward winter. The house got messier. Books piled up in odd places. Newspapers and magazines littered floors and tabletops. Dirty dishes sat in the sink until we ran out of plates and then someone washed them. Nobody did the laundry until we needed clean underwear or socks. Dust balls collected under beds and furniture and in the corners of rooms.

I spent more time in the woods. The weather was turning colder, and the tall trees rocked and swayed over my head, making that sad sound bare branches make when the wind blows through them. I could see the mountains now, ridge after ridge, blue in the distance.

I didn't worry about getting lost—I always carried a compass in my pocket—but sometimes the woods scared me. Maybe it was the solitude, maybe it was being in the presence of so many tall trees, but I'd find myself looking over my shoulder. I'd stop and listen. Branches sawed and scraped against each other. A twig snapped. The bushes rustled. I never saw anything, and I never told anyone, but sometimes I thought something was following me.

I'd think of the man—or whatever I'd seen—on the edge of the woods that night. I'd never seen him again, but what if he was following me, watching me from hidden places, waiting for the right opportunity to—to what? To kill me? Kidnap me? Harm me in some way?

I told myself not to be silly, it was just squirrels or birds rustling the bushes or the wind blowing high and lonesome over my head, but a little voice from a dark part of my mind kept whispering, *What if it's something else? What if it's something dangerous? What if Brody wasn't lying about the things in the woods?*

One afternoon I took the wrong trail and came out of the woods two or three miles down the road from our house. It was already late, and while I walked, the sun dropped below the top of the mountains. Soon I was stumbling along in the dark, wishing

I'd brought a flashlight, wishing I had a dog. I'd asked Dad if we could go to animal rescue and get one, but he said we couldn't afford an extra mouth to feed. He'd looked so depressed, I never asked again.

In the thick dark of the woods, I heard the rustling, snuffling sounds of a large animal nosing in the fallen leaves. I smelled something disgusting—rotten leaves, mildew, decay. A bear, it must be a bear. I'd seen black bears on my hikes, but never so near that I could smell them.

Just as I was about to run, I heard a car behind me. I moved to the edge of the road. An old Ford slowed to a stop. The driver rolled down his window.

"What are you doing out here all by yourself?" he asked. "It's getting dark, and look at you, wearing jeans and a black jacket. You're lucky I saw you."

I backed away. The man was a stranger, and I was alone on a dark road. He could grab me and throw me into his car and drive away.

Which was worse—being kidnapped or being attacked by a bear?

"You must be the kid who lives in the old Estes place," the man said. "You want a ride home?"

I shook my head. My feet were tangled up in vines, and I was scared that I was trapped. "That's okay. I like to walk," I stammered.

"In the dark? Who knows who might come along and get you?" Then he laughed. "Oh, I see, you think *I'm* going to get you. Is that it?"

He opened the car door. The overhead light came on, and I saw an old man with white hair. "I'm Mr. O'Neill from up the road a ways. I know your dad, Ted Anderson. Nice fella. Helps me carry stuff to my car at Home Depot. Come on, get in before you get yourself run over."

Mr. O'Neill looked harmless. He knew Dad's name and where he worked. "Thanks," I said. Lurching out of the vines, I slid into the car.

"What were you doing way out here?" he asked.

"Hiking," I told him. "I took the wrong turn on one of the trails."

"Lucky I came along. You won't catch me traipsing around in the woods all by my lonesome. Hasn't anybody told you about Bloody Bones?"

"Bloody Bones?" I laughed. "That's just a silly old scary story about a monster coming up the steps one at a time to get you."

"That's not the real story. Not by a long shot. There's a lot more to Bloody Bones than that." He peered at me. "You ever come across an old, fallen-down cabin up on a hill?"

"My dad and my sister and I went there once. Dad took pictures of it."

"Well, that cabin once belonged to Old Auntie. She was a conjure woman. You know what that is?"

"A witch?"

He nodded. "Well, Old Auntie lived by herself, save for this big old razorback hog she kept as a pet. She took that mean, ugly critter with her everywhere she went. Some folks said that hog walked on his hind legs like a man, and I believe he did."

He pulled into our driveway and let the engine idle. "Well, one day Old Auntie couldn't find her hog anywhere. She searched high, she searched low—no sign of him. So she got out her conjure pot and made a potion she could see things in. And you know what she saw?"

I shook my head.

"She saw this nasty old feller that lived up in the mountains. He'd been hunting razorback hogs. One of the hogs he caught was her pet. That sneaking, thieving rascal slaughtered all the hogs and skinned them and carved off their meat and threw what was left in a heap. In that pile, Old Auntie saw her hog's bald head and bloody bones. So she cast a spell to summon him back from the dead. His bones put themselves together and rose up on their hind feet. His skull jumped on top of the bones, and off he danced. On the way to the sneaking, thieving rascal's house, he got some claws from a dead bear, some teeth from a dead panther, and a tail from a dead raccoon."

Mr. O'Neill paused to look at his watch. "It's later than I thought. Guess I'll have to make a long story a mite shorter. The hog killed that lying, thieving rascal—tore him clean apart with the panther's teeth and ate him up. Then he dug his grave with the bear's claws and brushed the ground smooth with the raccoon's tail. He left that lying, thieving rascal's bones up there in the rocks all by himself. Folks round here say you can still hear him howling and moaning and screaming when the wind blows just right."

Even though I knew it was just a story, one I'd heard around a campfire at Boy Scout camp, Mr. O'Neill had a way of making it sound real. The dark woods and the lonely road and the wind swaying the treetops added a lot to the telling, or maybe it was because I was already half terrified, but the old man definitely had a knack for scaring people.

Trying to hide my fear, I asked him what happened to the hog.

"Well, he dressed himself in that lying, thieving rascal's overalls and went home to Old Auntie, raccoon tail and all."

He paused a moment. "From then on, he became known as Bloody Bones. There's not a child in this valley who's not scared of him."

"It's just an old story kids tell," I muttered, but my heart beat a little harder than normal at the idea of Bloody Bones. Suppose he was what I'd heard and smelled. What if he was just about to pounce on me when Mr. O'Neill came along and saved my life?

"And I tell you Bloody Bones still roams the woods," Mr. O'Neill said. "He got a liking for human flesh when he ate that lying, thieving rascal."

"Oh, sure." I tried hard not to look past the headlights into the unknowable dark surrounding the car. If Bloody Bones hid in the trees, I didn't want to see him.

"Don't you *Oh, sure* me, son." Mr. O'Neill looked hard at me. "To this day, people have a way of disappearing in these woods."

He leaned across me and opened the door. "You mind getting out here? I'm a little late for an appointment in town. Or would you rather I drive you all the way home?"

I sat in the brightly lit car. The headlights faded into the night a few feet up the driveway. The woods were dark, and the wind was blowing through treetops as bare as bones. Who knew what was out there?

"I walked pretty far today," I said in a low voice. "And I'm really tired. Would you mind driving me to the house?"

Mr. O'Neill chuckled and said he'd be glad to, seeing as how I was too tired to walk up the driveway. I could almost hear quotation marks around *tired*.

When the car stopped at the end of the driveway, I saw my sister looking out the window at us. She held Little Erica up so she could see, too.

"That your little sister?" he asked.

I nodded.

"She's a pretty little thing," he said. "Take good

care of her, son. Don't let her go wandering off like . . ." His voice trailed off.

"Like Selene?"

"Oh, you heard that story, did you?"

"From Brody Mason."

Mr. O'Neill sighed. "He's a sad case, that boy. His mama died a few months back, and he and his daddy are having a hard time. No telling what he'll tell you, but in the case of Selene, it's the honest-to-God truth."

"Did she really disappear?"

"Yes, she did. No one found her. No one knows what happened to her." He paused a moment. "Lord, that was fifty years ago."

"Did you know her?"

He nodded. "I knew the whole family. She and my daughter Eleanor were best friends. She played at our house or Eleanor played at her house almost every day. It just about broke Eleanor's heart when Selene vanished."

"What happened to the Estes family afterward?"

He sighed. "They moved about a year later. By then, they knew she wasn't coming back. We never knew where they went. After what happened, I reckon they didn't want anything to do with this place."

I had more questions, but Mr. O'Neill looked at his watch again and said, "Time for me to hit the road, son."

I got out of the car. "Thanks for the ride."

"Glad to do it. Say hi to your dad for me."

When I opened the kitchen door, Mom asked who brought me home.

"Mr. O'Neill. He knows Dad."

"He's a nice old fellow," Dad said. "I enjoy talking to him at work."

Mom frowned at me. "What have I told you about taking rides with strangers?"

"He wasn't a stranger, Mom. You heard Dad. He knows him."

"But *you* didn't know him," Mom said. "He could have been lying. He could have kidnapped you. Promise me you'll never do that again!"

"Now, Martha," Dad said. "We aren't in Connecticut anymore."

"No, we certainly aren't." With that, Mom yanked a frozen pizza out of the oven and called Erica to the table.

I was dying to ask Dad if Mr. O'Neill had ever told him about Bloody Bones, or if he'd talked to him about Selene Estes, but Erica was sitting across the table, picking at her food and smearing dabs on Little Erica's face. She had enough trouble sleeping without imagining Bloody Bones sneaking up the stairs to get her.

I figured it was best to keep quiet and eat my dinner. I'd ask Dad later, when he was alone.

But after dinner Dad secluded himself in his den. Mom stood at a living room window, a cigarette in her hand, and stared into the darkness. Erica sat on the couch and watched Mom. "Will you read to me, Mommy?" she asked.

"Not right now, Erica." Mom left the window and went to the kitchen.

My sister and I looked at each other. "She's crying," Erica said.

I sat down beside her. "I know."

"Nobody's happy anymore," Erica said.

"Yeah, I've noticed."

"It's this house. We never should have come here." She leaned toward me. "Do you ever feel like something bad will happen?"

I could have said *All the time, every minute,* but I kept my thoughts to myself. "Like what?" I asked.

Erica gazed past me into the fire blazing on the hearth. "I don't know, just something." She smoothed Little Erica's hair. "Those whispers," she added. "They're getting louder. They keep me awake at night. Are you sure you never hear them?"

"Like I told you, it's just the wind or the floorboards creaking. Old houses make lots of noises."

"The wind doesn't say people's names."

Mom came back and sat down beside Erica. Picking up *The Middle Moffat,* she asked, "What chapter are we on?"

As Mom began to read, I studied her face. Her eyes were red, and so was her nose. I wanted to ask her what was going on between her and Dad. Were they getting divorced? But I knew she'd say, *Don't be silly, Daniel. Nothing's wrong. Everyone has arguments sometimes.* That's the problem with families—too many things no one wants to talk about.

Since I wasn't interested in the Moffat family, I left Erica and Mom snuggled under a blanket and climbed the stairs to the second floor. Down the hall, a strip of light shone under Dad's door. I heard explosions and gunfire, which meant he was playing one of his war games.

Downstairs, Mom and Erica laughed about something Rufus Moffat said.

I'd never felt so alone in all my life.

The Dolly

It begins with a whisper in the dark, always the girl's name, always long and airy. The old woman blows it through keyholes and cracks. She guides it upstairs and down until it finds the girl's ear and nestles there. Air-ric-cah . . . No one can hear it but the girl.

The girl has trouble sleeping, she's fearful, she withdraws and spends most of her time with the dolly. Perfect. The old woman gives the dolly a sweet voice. The dolly uses her sweet voice to tell the girl she loves her, but no one else does. She tells the girl she understands how she feels, but no one else does. Especially her brother. He hates her, doesn't she know that? Hasn't she always known that?

The girl tells the doll how unhappy she is. The children at school are mean to her. They laugh at her clothes, they laugh at the way she talks. On the playground, they gather in groups and turn their backs. Her brother is mean to her too. Her parents pick on her. They love her brother more than they love her. The doll agrees with everything the girl tells her.

One day, when winter is closing in and the nights are long, the dolly tells the girl she wants to go to the woods. The girl is afraid of the woods, she never goes there. She stays inside by the fire where it's warm. She reads to the dolly, she talks to the dolly, she shares her unhappiness with the dolly.

But the dolly insists. She has secrets she will share with the girl, but only if they are outside in the woods where no one can hear and no one can see. "If you really love me," the dolly says, "you'll do as I ask. If you refuse me, I'll stop talking to you. I'll be what your brother says I am – a lump of plastic. Is that what you want?"

Of course it's not what the girl wants. She puts on her parka and her hat and her gloves, and she goes out into the cold with the dolly. The wind blows her name through the air. It's taken up by a flock of crows and passed on into the darkness – Air-ric-cah, Air-ric-cah . . .

The dolly shows her a path. "This must be a secret," she warns the girl. "You mustn't tell anyone what we see or do here."

And so it continues.

SIX

As the days passed, Erica and I spent less and less time together. While she spent her afternoons reading and drawing and playing with her stupid doll, I roamed the woods, exploring trails and searching for hawks. Thanks to my binoculars and Peterson's *Field Guide to Birds of North America,* I could identify red-tailed hawks, sharp-shinned hawks, and Cooper's hawks. I knew the difference between black buzzards and turkey buzzards. Once, I'd even seen a bald eagle.

At first I tried to persuade Erica to come with me, but she'd said no so often, I gave up asking. Fine.

Let her mope around the house with Little Erica. It was obvious she'd rather talk to a doll than to me. Pretty insulting, I thought.

On the school bus, we sat next to each other, but we didn't talk to each other and no one talked to us. Erica stared out the window, as if she expected to see something in the woods. I stared straight ahead, trying not to listen to the other kids laughing at the snobs from Connecticut.

One day after school I left the house in such a hurry I forgot my binoculars. I'd been watching a red-tailed hawk for a few days, and I needed the binoculars to see him in the woods. Annoyed at myself, I hurried home just in time to see my sister disappear into the woods on the other side of the house.

I stopped where I was, puzzled. Erica hated the woods—what was she up to? Maybe I should follow her and find out. Hadn't Mr. O'Neill told me to keep an eye on her?

Keeping a good distance between us, I walked as silently as if Erica were a bird I didn't want to frighten away. She'd taken a narrow path that meandered through the woods like a deer trail, circling around boulders and trees. Every now and then she stopped and stared into the underbrush as if she were looking for something.

Finally she came to a clearing and sat on a fallen tree. Cuddling her doll, she began whispering, just as if someone was with her—not the doll, but a person. I peered into the bushes around her, but I didn't see anyone. At least I don't *think* I did—it was more like I sensed a presence.

But no, that was crazy. All I heard was a whisper of wind prying leaves from branches. All I saw were shadows. I backed away from Erica. If she wanted to sit in the woods and hold imaginary conversations, let her. Why waste my afternoon spying on her?

Without making a sound, I crept away, retrieved my binoculars, and went in search of the red-tailed hawk.

By the time I came home, it was almost dark. Erica was sitting on the couch reading to Little Erica, exactly what she'd been doing when I'd left the house.

I lit the fire and sat beside her. "Have you been here all afternoon?"

She looked up from her book. "Of course. Where else would I be?"

"It's such a nice day, sunny and everything, I thought you might have gone outside to play for a while."

The doll regarded me with her usual blank stare, but Erica frowned at me. "You know I hate the woods."

I was about to accuse her of lying but then decided against it. Maybe I'd follow her again tomorrow, just in case I'd missed something.

Suddenly Erica leaned toward me and asked one of her typical out-of-nowhere questions. "Do you ever have secrets, Daniel?"

"Sometimes. Why? Do you?"

"Maybe," she said softly. She smiled and gazed into the fire.

"What do you mean 'maybe'? Either you do or you don't."

Instead of answering, Erica began reading to the doll again. " 'Once upon a time a woodcutter had two children, a boy named Hansel and a girl named Gretel—' "

"About your secret," I said, "the one you may or may not have. Has it got anything to do with the woods?"

"I'm reading to Little Erica now," my sister said. "Don't interrupt me."

I wanted to snatch the book out of her hands and throw it into the corner and hurl the doll after it. Instead, I left my sister and the doll on the couch and went to the kitchen to make myself a peanut butter sandwich. As I ate, I heard Erica reading "'Nibble nibble, mousekin'" in a scary witch's voice, much deeper and raspier than her normal voice. I almost got up to see if someone else was in the living room.

The Secret

The old woman waits in the woods, but you wouldn't recognize her. She has taken the form of the girl in the cabin. She watches Erica sit down on a log, just where the dolly tells her to sit. Good. The girl is biddable. She does as she's told.

The old woman comes closer. She smiles shyly and waits for Erica to notice her.

"Who are you?" Erica is startled, but not afraid, as she would be if the old woman had come as herself.

The old woman wears a gray plaid dress with a round collar. Her hair is red and curly. Her face is sweet and sad.

"I come to be your friend." The old woman speaks in a soft, childish voice that soothes the girl.

"I don't have any friends," Erica whispers.

"You got yourself one now." The girl sits on the log beside Erica. "That's a mighty pretty dolly you got. Can I hold her?"

Erica holds the dolly tighter. "She's very special."

"Please." The girl reaches for the dolly. "I ain't never seen a dolly so pretty as that."

Erica looks distrustful, but the dolly whispers, "Let her hold me, it's all right."

Reluctantly, Erica hands the little girl her dolly.

"Oh, I wish I had me a dolly like this one," the little girl says.

Rocking the doll in her arms, she croons a little song. The tune is familiar, but Erica can't make out the words.

Later, when Erica goes home, she doesn't remember what happened in the woods. It's a secret, even from herself.

After that, the old woman in her little-girl shape meets Erica in the woods every day. She tells her she lives with her sweet old auntie in a pretty little cabin on the tippity top of a hill. "She loves me ever so much," the old woman says in the little-girl voice. "More'n anybody ever did."

"More than your mommy and daddy?" Erica asks.

"My mama and daddy never loved me. They made me work hard at chores and beat me black-and-blue and made me sleep on the floor by the fireplace 'cause I was so bad."

"My parents would never do that."

"Oh yes, they would. Parents never love their little ones. They can't wait to get rid of them. You'll see. One day they'll get fed up with you and start treating you bad, just the way mine did."

Erica stares at her, and the little girl smiles. Things are going well. Erica believes everything the girl tells her. "They already love your brother more than you."

"It's true," Erica says. "They've always loved Daniel best."

"My auntie's keeping an eye on you," the little girl says in her sweet little, false little voice. "She loves you even though you don't know it yet, and she aims to rescue you and bring you to her cabin, where me and you will live like sisters."

The little girl pats Erica's hand. "Come live with us

afore they start into beating you and scolding you and making you sleep by the fire. Why, they could kill you dead one night."

Erica draws back a little. "You're scaring me."

The little girl says, "There ain't nothing to be scared of. Come away with me, and I'll keep you safe."

"Will I have to go to school?"

"School? No indeed. Old Auntie got no use for school. She'll teach you all you need to know."

Erica nods her head. Yes, she'll come with the little girl. And stay with her and Old Auntie. And never go to school again. Maybe not today, maybe not tomorrow. But soon.

The old woman sees the brother watching from the woods. He can't see her, but he knows someone is there. "I must go," she whispers to Erica, and slips away into the woods.

SEVEN

The next day, I left the house with my binoculars and my bird book, but instead of going to the woods, I hid in the tall weeds near the house and waited. It was a colder day and windy, but in a few minutes Erica ran out the back door, darted across the yard, and disappeared into the woods.

She took the same path, turned off into the clearing, and sat on the fallen tree. Her bright blue scarf blew in the wind, and her red hair swirled.

Hiding behind a tall maple, I watched her closely. Once in a while she whispered to the doll, but for the most part she neither moved nor spoke. She sat still and stared into the woods—waiting, I thought, but for what? Definitely a girl with secrets. No "maybes" about it.

The wind yanked the last of the leaves from the trees and sent them flying through the air. They rustled and sighed and sank to the ground in brown and yellow heaps. Some settled in Erica's hair and on her shoulders. Others landed on Little Erica.

Nothing distracted my sister. Not the falling leaves. Not the squirrel chattering on a branch over her head. Not the crow cawing from the top of a dead tree. She sat so still, I thought she must be holding her breath.

Suddenly she stood up and took a step or two toward the dead tree. She held the doll tightly and whispered to her.

While I watched Erica, I glimpsed a shadow drifting toward her through the trees—dark and formless, like a wisp of fog or smoke. I couldn't tell what it was—an old woman, a little girl, an animal—something small and dangerous, I could sense it. Behind it was something else, something worse, a shadowy, bony thing, taller than a man.

"Erica!" I shouted. "Stop, don't go near it! Run!"

My sister turned to me. "Daniel! What are you doing here?"

The shadow, or whatever it was, vanished, but I grabbed Erica and started pulling her away. "What's wrong with you? Can't you see? There was something there!"

"Let me go!" she screamed. "Let me go!"

"No. You're coming home, right now!"

"My doll," she cried, "my doll."

Little Erica lay on the ground where my sister had dropped her, her face in the leaves.

"I have to get her!" Erica twisted and turned, kicking me, flailing her arms. "She wants her! She'll take her!"

"Who wants her?" I yelled. "Who'll take her?"

Erica didn't answer, but she struggled even harder to get away from me, crying and screaming. Holding her was like holding a cat that doesn't want to be held. She didn't have claws or sharp teeth, but she managed to bite me twice and scratch my face.

But I didn't let her go. And I didn't pick up the doll.

Out of the woods at last, I saw Mom and Dad

getting out of the van. When they saw me hauling Erica through the weeds, they hurried toward us.

"What's going on?" Dad shouted. "Are you all right?"

With a burst of strength, Erica broke away and ran to Mom and began a sobbing account of what happened. "I was playing in the woods," she cried, "and all of a sudden Daniel grabbed me and started dragging me home. He said I wasn't allowed to be in the woods. He made me leave Little Erica there — she's lying on the ground all by herself."

Dad and Mom looked at each other. "You take care of Daniel," Mom said to him. "I'll get Erica into the house. She's hysterical."

"No." Erica began struggling again. "I have to get Little Erica. I can't leave her there!"

"It's almost dark," Dad said. "We'll get the doll tomorrow."

"No, no! I'll never see her again." Erica thrashed about wildly, more like a cat than before.

"Take her to the house, Ted," Mom cried. "I can't hold her!"

Dad got a firm grip on Erica, picked her up,

and carried her toward the house. Her shrieks finally stopped when the back door closed behind Dad.

Mom turned to me. "What's this about? Why wouldn't you let her get the doll?"

"There was something in the woods, something dark and scary." Words tumbled out of my mouth. I didn't think about what I was saying. I didn't try to stop myself. "I had to get her away from it."

Mom looked at me as if I'd lost my mind. "What are you talking about?"

"I don't know. I saw it. I was scared. I thought it was going to grab Erica. She was just standing there, like she was paralyzed or something."

Mom put her hands on my shoulders and gave me a little shake. "Daniel, how often do I need to tell you? No one is going to take you or Erica. No one is going to disappear."

I took a deep breath and tried to calm down. I wanted to believe Mom. I hadn't seen anything in the woods. Neither had Erica. It was all my imagination. Selene Estes had disappeared, but she hadn't been taken by Bloody Bones. He was a legend, he wasn't real. I couldn't have seen him.

But no matter what I told myself, I knew I'd seen

something. I couldn't explain it. I didn't know what it was, but it had been there.

After Erica cried herself to sleep, I talked Dad into going to the woods with flashlights to look for the doll. I didn't want to leave the house, but I felt bad about leaving Little Erica in the woods. That doll was just a hunk of plastic to me, but to Erica she was almost a real person.

When we opened the back door, a gust of wind blew leaves into the kitchen. They skittered across the floor and settled in corners as if they'd been waiting to come inside.

It took all of Dad's strength to pull the door shut behind us. The night was biting cold. An almost full moon lit the field.

At the edge of the woods, we turned on our flashlights. The wind tossed the trees, and their shadows danced over the path, crossing and crisscrossing the ground, making it hard to see.

I stayed close to Dad and aimed the flashlight at the ground. Nothing looked familiar. It was as if we'd taken a different path, one you could find only at night. I heard noises in the undergrowth. I imagined creatures you'd never see in daylight scurrying through the dead leaves. I kept my eyes on the path so I wouldn't see anything in the shadows on either side of me.

After we'd walked for half an hour or so, Dad stopped. His flashlight probed the dark, picking out one tree, then another. An owl was caught in the beam for a moment, its eyes huge and shining. Without giving me time to identify him, he flew soundlessly into the woods.

"Are you sure we're going the right way?" Dad asked.

"I think maybe we passed the clearing," I admitted. "I don't remember it being this far."

"I told you we should wait until morning to look for that doll."

I shone my flashlight behind us. "It all looks the same in the dark."

"So I noticed," Dad said.

We turned around and walked back the way we'd come. Dad studied every tree, every boulder, every fallen log.

He asked the same questions over and over. "Is this it? Does that tree look familiar? Do you think we're close?"

My answer was always the same. "I don't know."

After a while, Dad came up with new questions. "Did you scare Erica on purpose? Why didn't you stop and let her get the doll? Were you teasing her? Bullying her?"

"No," I said. "No. I saw something, Dad. I thought—"

He shook his head. "You *saw* something. All this because you *saw* something. What's wrong with you? I've been all over these woods and never seen anything out of the ordinary."

Bumbling and stumbling ahead of me, Dad thrashed at dry weeds and dead vines with a stick. Everything was my fault—my fault Erica was hysterical, my fault the doll was missing, my fault we couldn't find the clearing, my fault we were wandering around in the woods freezing our butts off.

"I give up," Dad said. "The doll's gone, and your sister is heartbroken. You should feel really great about that."

Dad had never talked to me this way. He got mad so easily now. So did Mom. Erica was unhappy and secretive and strange. I was miserable in school. And lonely. Nothing was right.

Without speaking to each other, Dad and I left the woods and trudged across the field. In the cold and windy dark, the house looked warm and inviting. Lights shone from the windows, smoke rose from the chimney, but it was like a mirage. Up close, inside the house, the warmth and happiness vanished.

No one spoke at breakfast. Mom slammed bowls of cold cereal down in front of Erica and me. She and Dad had already eaten and were getting ready to leave for work.

Before she left, Mom hugged Erica. "Please don't look so sad, sweetie. You and Daniel can look for Little Erica when you get home from school. In the daylight, you're sure to find her."

Erica didn't say anything. She sat with her head down, her cereal untouched, tears trickling down her cheeks.

"Erica, I promise I'll find her," I said. "I don't know what got into me. I thought—"

"That's enough, Daniel," Mom said. "Forget about what you thought you saw in the woods. You're just making matters worse."

"But Mom—"

Outside, Dad blew the horn, already annoyed.

"I have to leave." Mom grabbed her purse and fumbled with the zipper on her parka. The horn blew again.

"All right, all right," Mom muttered. To me she said, "Find the doll. Erica's very upset. She cried all night."

The door slammed shut, and the van drove away, its tires spraying gravel. I took Erica's untouched cereal and put our bowls and glasses in the sink. "We have to leave in ten minutes," I reminded her.

She nodded, but she didn't move from the table.

"Aren't you going to brush your teeth?"

No response. I did what I had to do in the bathroom and returned to find Erica sitting exactly where I'd left her.

I took her parka and mine off the hook. "Here, put this on."

Erica got up slowly and allowed me to help her with her jacket. "You should at least comb your hair," I told her. "You look terrible."

"Who cares what I look like?" Erica pulled on her mittens and a knit cap Mom had made for her. "Everyone at school hates me."

"Where are your schoolbooks?"

"I don't know."

I looked around and saw her book bag on the floor by the front door. From its weight, I knew her books were inside. "Did you do your homework?"

"No." Erica slipped the straps over her shoulder and followed me outside. The wind was cold and damp and smelled of winter.

Silently we walked down the driveway. Now that the trees were bare, we could see farther into the woods, all the way to the road.

"Erica," I said, "did you see anything in the woods? A sort of dark shape, a shadow maybe?"

"No."

"But you were sitting on that log, staring into the woods as if you were talking to somebody. And then you got up and walked straight toward whatever it was."

She shook her head. "That's what *you* thought I was doing."

"Well, what were you doing?"

"Nothing."

I wanted to shake the truth out of her, but I took a deep breath, counted to ten, and finally said, "You told me you had a secret. Is it something you do in the woods? Someone you see? Or talk to? Do you still hear whispers in the dark?"

Erica looked at me at last, her pale face closed tight. "A secret is something you don't tell anyone, Daniel. That's what it means."

"Does Mom know?"

"I just told you. It's only a secret if you don't tell anyone." With that, Erica ran down the driveway ahead of me.

I picked up a stone and threw it into the woods as far as I could. *Thonk*. It hit a tree and bounced off. I was frustrated. No matter what I asked, Erica would not give me an answer. Somehow, my seven-year-old sister was getting the best of me.

I caught up with her at the end of the driveway. Shivering in the wind, we waited silently for the bus. I'd given up talking to her. What was the point?

EIGHT

As soon as we boarded the bus, Mrs. Plummer noticed Erica's mood. "What's the matter, sweetie? You get up on the wrong side of the bed or something?"

Or something, I thought.

"It's my doll, Little Erica, you know—the one I told you about. My brother made me leave her in the woods, and now she's gone."

Mrs. Plummer turned around and looked directly at me. "Why on earth did you do something like that?"

As usual, I was being blamed. "It's kind of complicated," I said. "I thought, well, I won't tell you what I thought. It's dumb, and you wouldn't believe me. Let's just say I made a mistake, and I'm really sorry and I'll find the doll after school."

"He won't find her no matter how hard he looks." Erica turned her face to the window and pressed her nose against the glass. "She's been took," Erica whispered to herself in a voice so low I scarcely heard her.

Mrs. Plummer looked at me in the rearview mirror. "What makes you think I won't believe you?"

"My parents don't." She was slowing down to pick up Brody. With him getting on the bus, I couldn't tell her what I saw.

"Tell me later," Mrs. Plummer told me.

As usual, Brody gave me a nasty look as he walked past. He was heading for a seat at the back of the bus where he and his friends sat.

Ignoring him, I looked straight ahead, and Erica looked out the window. We rode in silence all the way to school.

My day was no worse than usual. A B-minus on a history report because I'd gotten a date wrong. A bloody nose in basketball—an accident of course. And so on and so on.

The bus ride home *was* worse than usual because

Erica still refused to speak to me. Without her to talk to, I had to listen to rude comments about my sweater, my haircut, my shoes, and who knows what. I wondered how the kids on the bus had entertained themselves before I'd had the bad luck to move to Woodville.

After Brody got off, Mrs. Plummer glanced at us in the rearview mirror once or twice, but she didn't have anything to say until she stopped at the end of our driveway. "I hope you find the doll, but be quick about it. It gets dark early, and I don't want you getting lost in the woods."

She shut the door and drove away, heading home, I guessed, to her husband and kids. We stood at the side of the road and looked down the driveway. The trees were a tunnel of darkness already.

"Let's go straight to the woods and look for your doll," I said.

"She won't be there," Erica said in the flat little voice she'd been using all day.

"Yes, she will." I took her hand to hurry her along, but she pulled away and ran ahead.

I chased her through the field's tall weeds and into the woods. In a few minutes I came to the dead tree, the clearing, and the fallen log. How had Dad and I missed it last night?

Erica waited for me, empty-handed. "She's not here."

"She must be." I ran around looking in piles of fallen leaves, under bushes, behind logs, even leaving the clearing to search the woods.

Erica stayed where she was, her arms folded across her chest, shivering.

"I don't understand it." I pointed to the place where I'd last seen Little Erica. "She was right there." I kicked at the leaves, scattering them, thinking the doll had to be under them.

Erica hugged herself as if she still held the doll in her arms. "She's been took."

"'Took'? That's how the kids in Woodville talk, not you and me. We say 'taken.' And besides, who took her?"

"Selene." The name dropped from Erica's lips like a stone. "The girl who lives on the tippity top of a hill with her old auntie."

"Are you crazy or just a liar? Selene disappeared fifty years ago. Nobody's seen her since."

Honestly, I wasn't as sure as I tried to sound. My

feeling of being watched, the darkness of the woods surrounding the house, Erica's behavior, the tension between Mom and Dad, the unhappiness we'd all sunk into—everything was wrong. Maybe, just maybe, it all tied in with Selene Estes. Or something else—I didn't know what.

My brain was muddled. My hands and nose were cold, and I wanted to go home, light the fire, and play games on my iPad.

Erica stared into the woods, at the very spot where I'd seen, or thought I'd seen, the shadow thing.

"You saw something yesterday," I said. "I know it."

"Suppose I did?" Erica's pale face looked spooky in the dim light, her eyes too big for her face and shadowed with dark circles.

"What did you see?" I stood over her. "I want to know!"

"It's a secret. I made a promise, I—" She was crying now.

Angry and frustrated by her silent, secret ways, I pulled her to her feet and shook her. Not hard, just a little. "I'm serious. There's something going on, and I need to know what it is."

"Let me go, let me go!" Erica struggled to get

away. It was just like the day before, and I was fed up.

"Tell me!" I shouted. "Tell me the truth, you little liar!" I let go of her and shoved her so hard she fell on her back in the leaves.

Scrambling to her feet, she glared at me like a wild thing. Her hair hung in her face; leaves clung to her jacket. "I hate you, Daniel! No matter what you do, you can't make me tell. Never never never!"

She spun around and dashed into the woods.

"Come back here!" I yelled.

I ran after her, slipping and sliding on fallen leaves, tripping on roots hidden beneath the leaves. A branch she'd brushed aside flew back and hit my eye. Its thorns clawed my face.

Smarting from pain, I shouted, "Go on, then, stupid! Run. You'll be sorry if you get lost and it's dark and cold and . . ." I stopped yelling because I couldn't hear her crashing through the bushes anymore.

Fine, I thought. *I brought her home yesterday. I'm not doing it again. Let her find her own way back, maybe it'll teach her a lesson.*

I turned away and followed the path back to the house. It was practically dark, and a cold wind hissed through the dry weeds. Erica wouldn't stay long in the woods. She probably knew a shortcut. When I got home, she'd be there, sitting on the couch, smirking because she'd beaten me. Mom would never know I'd let my sister run off into the woods without me.

The Taking

The old woman returns to the clearing and waits for Erica and her hateful brother. She leaves the dolly hidden in the woods near her cabin. She has another use for it.

She hears them coming before she sees them. Their voices are loud and angry.

The hateful brother can't believe the doll is gone, but Erica knows who took it. *That girl,* she tells him. *The one who lives with her auntie on the tippity top of a hill.* They fight, and the hateful brother pushes his sister. She falls backward into the leaves. Now she knows he hates her. She must find the cabin and the girl.

She scrambles to her feet and runs away from him. The old woman makes sure he gives up and goes home.

She lets Erica run until she's too tired to go farther. She watches Erica sink down on the ground and cry. She waits until the trees thicken with shadows. The wind blows harder, its breath as cold as death. Bloody Bones snuffles and snorts in the dead leaves, looking for grubs or voles, anything juicy or crunchy.

Erica hears him coming closer, step by shuffling step. She whimpers and cries and curls herself into a ball.

When the old woman is sure that Erica cannot run or put up a fight, she steps out of the woods in her own shape. Her ragged cloak billows around her gnarled body. Strands of white hair stream across her bony face. She stands over Erica, leaning on her staff, older than old, crueler than cruel, as wicked as the devil hisself.

"Air-ric-cah," she croons. "Air-ric-cah, come to Auntie."

Erica looks up. The old woman takes her arm and pulls her roughly to her feet. "You belong to me now. No one wants you but me, no one loves you but me. They've forgot all about you, and you've forgot all about them."

Smiling to herself, the old woman drags Erica through the woods to her cabin. She has what she wants.

NINE

When I slammed into the kitchen, Erica wasn't there. I called out, just in case, but there's something about an empty house. You always know when you're alone.

I pictured her taking her time coming home, sulking, mad, hoping I'd worry about her. Little brat. I couldn't stand my sister anymore. I was sick of her. Sick of her scenes. Sick of the doll. I hoped we'd never find it.

I smeared a thick layer of peanut butter on a piece of bread, poured myself a glass of cider, and went to my room to play games on my iPad. But for some reason I couldn't concentrate. The silence of the house pressed against my ears. A clock ticked. The refrigerator turned off and on. A gust of wind rattled the windowpanes. Noises you never heard except when there were no other noises.

I closed my iPad and went to the window. Where was Erica? I walked down the hall to her room. Maybe she'd been hiding there all the time, playing a trick on me. Yes, that must be it. She'd beaten me home, run upstairs, and hidden. It was just the sort of prank she'd pull.

Fully expecting to see her sitting on her bed, laughing at me, I flung open the door and flicked on the light. A row of stuffed animals sat on the window seat, staring at me with shiny round eyes.

I called my sister's name. I looked under her bed and in the closet, expecting her to jump out and scare me. No Erica.

As I turned to leave the room, I saw the van's headlights coming down the driveway. With a half-formed hope that Erica would be with Mom and Dad, I ran down the back stairs to the kitchen and opened the door before Dad had a chance to fumble with his key.

"Well, thanks, buddy." Dad brushed past me and set a case of wine down on the counter with a thud.

Mom was right behind him, balancing a stack of carryout cartons from Lucky's Chinese Restaurant. "No pizza tonight. Moo goo gai pan for you and me and Erica."

"And General Tso's chicken for me." Dad turned to the cupboard to get dinner plates. "Go fetch Erica so we can eat before the won ton soup gets cold."

"Why are you just standing there?" Mom asked. "What's wrong? Where's Erica?"

"She—" I took a deep breath, then started again. "She's not, she's, she's not—"

Mom left the kitchen. "Erica," she called. "Erica!"

Dad grabbed my shoulders and spun me around to face him. "What's going on, Daniel? Where's your sister?"

"She's not here, Dad. I don't know where she is. We had a fight. She wouldn't come home with me— she, she ran off—"

"She *ran off*?" Dad stared at me. "Why didn't you go after her? How could you let her run off?"

,"I tried to stop her, Dad, but she was mad just like yesterday, and I—"

His eyes lit on the jar of peanut butter and the loaf of bread I'd forgotten to put away. "You came home and ate a sandwich? Is that what you did?"

"I thought she'd be here any minute. I never imagined she'd do something like this."

Mom reappeared. "She's not in the house, Ted."

Dad grabbed my shoulders again, harder this time. "Where did you last see her?"

"In the clearing. We were looking for the doll, but she wasn't there, and Erica wouldn't come home with me. She got mad. She said it was all my fault, and then she ran away from me, and I got mad at her and came home."

Dad swore softly. "Martha, you stay here in case she comes back. Daniel, grab your jacket and a couple of flashlights."

I followed Dad out into the cold, dark night. The wind was blowing harder now, and the trees sent wild rocking shadows across the driveway. In the woods, Dad began calling Erica. I joined in.

Erica, Erica, Erica. Her name bounced from tree

to tree, caught by the wind, tossed into the sky. But she didn't answer. She didn't come.

"Where are you?" Dad called, his voice scraped raw from shouting.

Are you, are you, are you, the trees repeated. Creatures in the underbrush rustled. An owl screeched.

Our voices sounded small in the noisy darkness.

We called her name again and again. We waved our flashlights in hope that she'd see their bobbing light. We were hoarse from calling. And desperate when she didn't answer.

The faint trail gave out, and we began circling back to the house without realizing it until we saw the lights in the windows.

"We need to call the police," Dad said. "We don't know the land the way they do. We'll get lost ourselves if we keep going."

Wordlessly, we made our way home. Mom was on the front porch, shivering in her warmest down coat. "You didn't find her?"

"No." Dad stopped to hug her. Mom clung to him. They stood there whispering to each other, as if they'd forgotten about me. I waited, shifting my weight from one frozen foot to the other, afraid Bloody Bones might be watching us from the trees.

Not that I believed he actually existed, not in my world, the real world, the five-senses world. But with the wind blowing and the moon sailing in and out of clouds like a ghost racing across the sky, I could almost believe I'd crossed a border into another world, where anything could be true—even conjure women and spells and monsters.

The police came sooner than we'd expected. We heard their sirens and saw their flashing lights before they'd even turned into the driveway. Four cars and an ambulance stopped at the side of the house. Doors opened, men got out. A couple of them had dogs, big German shepherds who pulled on their leashes, excited. Flashing lights washed the living room walls with red and blue.

"Why did they bring an ambulance?" Mom clung to Dad, her face a strange ashen color.

He frowned at the scene outside. "It's standard procedure when something like this happens."

Something like what? I wondered. No one was hurt. We didn't need an ambulance. Unless they thought—but no, Erica wasn't hurt, she was just lost. They'd find her fast with those dogs. I'd tell her I was sorry I got mad at her. I was scared, that was all. Scared of what? An old folktale? I shivered as a draft of cold air came creeping into the house. At my age, how could I be scared of a bogeyman?

Two policemen came inside and went upstairs. I heard their shoes clunking overhead. A policewoman sat down with us at the dining room table. She had questions: Erica's full name and age, a description of her and the clothes she was wearing, and the circumstances of her disappearance.

"Daniel was supposed to walk home from the school-bus stop with Erica," Mom said in a shaky voice, "but they had a fight, and, and—" She faltered and tried to brush away her tears.

The detective turned to me. "What was the fight about?" She'd been jotting things in a little notebook, and now she sat looking at me, waiting, her pen poised. She had stubby fingers and close-cut fingernails, no polish. No makeup either. A plain face, short hair. Not very friendly. Small, hard eyes. The name on her badge said Detective Irma Shank.

I told her what I'd told Dad, still leaving out any

mention of things in the woods or Selene Estes. My hands shook, and one leg jiggled without my being able to stop it.

"So he came home and ate a peanut butter sandwich," Mom said when I'd finished. "Then I imagine he went upstairs to play a game on his iPad. When we came home, he panicked and told us what happened."

While Mom talked, Detective Shank watched me, still jotting things down. "Is that what you did, Daniel?"

"Yes, but I thought Erica was playing a trick on me. She does things like that."

She looked at Dad and Mom, and they nodded. "Sometimes Erica is very willful," Dad said. "She's not happy here."

I wanted to say, *That goes for all of us,* but I kept my mouth shut.

"Where did you live before you moved here?"

"Fairfield, Connecticut," Dad said.

Detective Shank leaned across the table. "I know your daughter's only seven, but do you think she'd try to go back there?"

Dad and Mom looked at each other and shook their heads. None of us could picture Erica going to Connecticut. She had no money, and even if she did, what ticket seller would let her get on a bus all by herself?

"She's high-strung, fearful," Mom said. "I can't imagine her being outside in the dark—she's *afraid* of the dark. She sleeps with a light on." Now Mom began to cry in earnest. "She must be so scared. And so cold."

A policeman came inside. "We need something Erica has worn recently so we can set the dogs on her trail."

"And a recent photograph," Detective Shank added.

Dad went upstairs and came back with a pair of red socks Erica had worn the day before. Mom gave the police one of a recent set of school photographs.

"Beautiful little girl," Detective Shank said. "But such a sad expression." She looked at us with narrowed eyes, as if she were blaming us for everything.

The policeman went outside with the socks.

Through the window, I saw the dogs sniff the socks before the police led them into the field.

"I can't believe this is happening," Mom said. "It's like a nightmare."

"I know. I know." The detective patted Mom's hand. "Would you like tea?"

Mom nodded, and the woman went to the kitchen.

"Make yourself useful, Daniel," Dad said. "Show her where things are."

"Please don't blame me for this, Dad."

Dad looked around the room. "I don't see anyone else to blame."

In the kitchen, I went to the cabinet over the stove and got out cups and saucers. Detective Shank had already found tea bags and put the kettle on the stove.

While we waited for the water to boil, she looked at me. "When you and Erica were fighting, did you hit Erica, Daniel? Knock her down or hurt her somehow?"

Her question really upset me. Did she suspect me of harming Erica in some way or leaving her unconscious in the woods?

"I shoved her," I admitted, "and she fell down, but not hard. She jumped up and ran away from me."

"Are you sure that's all you did?"

"I'd never hurt my sister."

"Of course you wouldn't. Not on purpose." She looked at my face closely and touched the scratches on my cheek. "Did Erica do this?"

"It was a branch. She pushed it out of her way, and it swung back and hit me. The thorns scratched me, not my sister."

"What were you fighting about?"

"I told you. She was mad about the doll. She said it was my fault it was gone."

"Why did you prevent Erica from picking up the doll yesterday?"

"It was almost dark. We had to go home."

"I don't understand what difference it would have made to pick up the doll."

I started crying. I couldn't help it. "I should have let her get the doll. She really loves it. I wish I had, but I, I—I don't like being in the woods when it's dark."

The teakettle started whistling while I was trying to explain. Mom heard it, I guess, and came to the door. "What's going on?" she asked the detective. "Daniel's a minor. You have no right to question him without my permission."

"I'm just trying to understand why the doll was left in the woods yesterday, ma'am. It seems peculiar."

Mom turned off the stove, and the kettle's shrill whistle stopped. She put an arm around me, and I leaned against her, incredibly grateful for her protection. I'd begun to think that my whole family, as well as everyone else in Woodville, hated me, including Detective Irma Shank.

"I was scared," I finally admitted. "I was scared to stop for the doll."

"What were you afraid of?" Detective Shank shook her head, as if she didn't believe me. "You don't look like the sort of boy who's easily scared."

"I thought I saw something in the woods, in the shadows," I told her. "I was scared it was coming after Erica and me."

Detective Shank seemed unconvinced. Probably she'd already decided I had more to do with Erica's disappearance than I was saying.

Mom spoke up. "The children have been nervous, anxious. They're not used to living in the country with no neighbors. It's so dark at night. They're imaginative. They, they—"

Mom held me tighter. She was crying again. "Daniel has told you all he knows. Please spend your time searching for Erica. She's out there in the cold, and you're sitting here questioning Daniel as if you suspect him of harming his sister."

Detective Shank got to her feet. "Children often know more than they let on," she said with a glance at me. "I'm trying to understand all the aspects, ma'am. Believe me, I want to find your daughter as much as you do."

With that, the detective left the house and joined the police, who were now searching the shed.

"Do you still want tea, Mom?"

She nodded, and I made us both a cup. "Do you think Dad wants one?"

"He's outside, no doubt making a nuisance of himself." Cup in hand, she went to the window and stared past the reflection of the kitchen into the darkness beyond. "Where can she be, Daniel?"

Suddenly Dad barged into the kitchen with a couple of cops. He was holding Erica's knit hat, the one she'd worn yesterday. "One of the dogs found it caught on a branch," he said, "about a mile from here. A mile! How could she have gone that far?"

Mom took the hat and pressed it to her face. Crying softly, she continued to gaze into the darkness beyond the window.

"Where are the dogs?" I asked. "Are they still on Erica's trail?"

Dad gestured toward the squad cars and the ambulance still parked near the house. "Out there. They lost her scent not long after they found the hat."

I stared at Dad. "But they'll find her, right?"

"Yes, of course. Tomorrow they'll ask for volunteers to form lines and search the woods. It'll be better in the daylight. They can . . ." His voice dropped, and he stared out the window. "I can't believe this."

Before the police left, the officer in charge told us to get some sleep, to hope for the best. Erica was probably lost, but with the help of volunteer searchers, they'd find her tomorrow.

I can't speak for my parents, but I doubt they

slept much that night. I certainly didn't. For hours, I sat at my bedroom window, willing Erica to find her way out of the woods.

I'll never tease you again or get mad at you, I promised. *Just come home. Please, Erica, please come home. I'm so, so sorry.*

TEN

In the gray light of dawn I woke to the sound of voices in the kitchen. Mom was serving coffee to the volunteers who had brought doughnuts and Danish pastries and sticky buns. The whole house smelled like sugar, but I had no appetite for any of it.

Mom gave me a cup of hot chocolate. "Drink it," she said. "It's cold outside. Take some doughnuts or something."

She was pale, her eyes red and puffy from crying, and she was smoking. A woman from the Realtor's office told her to go back to bed, she looked terrible, but Mom insisted she was fine. "We're going to find Erica today," she said.

To please Mom, I took a doughnut and went outside. The police were talking to a bunch of people I didn't know, telling them what was expected of them. Form lines, walk an arm's length apart, examine every inch of ground. "If you see anything that may be connected with Erica, stop and call a policeman. Do not move it, do not touch it, leave it *in situ,* and wait for a policeman."

I edged away toward the woods. No one noticed me go. I had a crazy idea I could find Erica myself, be a hero, make up for leaving the doll and all that it had led to.

In the clearing where I'd last seen my sister, a crow perched in the dead tree. He cocked his head at me, cawed, and flew away. I sat down on the log and tried to think about where Erica might have gone.

I sat there for a while, but no ideas came to me. I stood up and called her, again and again, until my voice was as hoarse and raspy as a crow's. Her name rang in the air, bounced from tree to tree, echoed back to me. But she didn't answer. Nor did she come running out of the woods, her red curls in a tangle, her parka muddy—breathless, cold, hungry, elated to see me, Daniel, her rescuer.

"You won't find her that way."

I spun around, startled to see Brody standing a few feet away. He wore a ratty fringed suede jacket that looked as if it had once belonged to his mother. His bony knees stuck out of holes in his jeans, and his hair straggled over his eyes.

"What are you doing here?" I asked him.

"My dad's in the search party, so I thought I'd come along over and see what's going on. I heard you calling your sister's name. I doubt she'll hear you, no matter how loud you yell."

"She might hear me. Nobody knows how far away she is. She could be trying to find her way home right now. She could have fallen into a hole or something."

He edged closer to me, shuffling through leaves as he came. "Listen," he said in a low voice, "there's stuff about this place you don't know, stuff nobody's told you, mainly because you're such a stuck-up snot."

I stared at him suspiciously. His nose was running, and his eyes had a moist, pink look. If I was such a stuck-up snot, what did he want with me? Why was he here?

"What kind of stuff?" I found myself lowering my voice too.

He shrugged and took a quick look around. His eyes lingered on the dead tree. "You know what happened to Selene Estes, right?"

"You told me about her. Remember? On the bus—the first day I came to school."

Brody was almost whispering now. He kept looking at the dead tree. "Well, folks are saying your sister's been took, just like Selene was. And you won't ever see her again."

Took—there was that word again—how had Erica picked it up?

"Don't be so stupid, Brody. Selene disappeared more than fifty years ago. Whoever took her is dead by now—and so is Selene."

"Maybe," Brody said, "maybe not."

"Next you'll be telling me Bloody Bones took her."

"Nah, Old Auntie's got her. Ask anybody in Woodville. They'll tell you."

"Old Auntie lived a long time ago," I said. "She's definitely dead. If she even existed—which I doubt."

Brody shook his head. "She lives way back in the woods, up on Brewster's Hill. Every now and then somebody sees her at night, walking along the highway, collecting dead things. Her and Bloody Bones. That's what they eat. Roadkill."

"I don't believe you."

"You want me to take you to her cabin?" Brody asked, his eyes still boring into mine. "That's where everybody thinks she kept Selene. Maybe that's where your sister's at."

"I know where it is. I've been there with Dad and Erica. It's an old, falling-down ruin—nobody lives in it."

"In the daytime, yeah, but at night it looks like it used to."

"That's crazy," I said.

"I'm going up there," he said. "You can come if you like. Or not. Makes no matter to me what you do." He turned and started walking away.

I followed him. The fringe on his jacket blew

in the wind. The little beads sewed to it rattled and bumped together.

"What do you mean at night it's like it used to be?" I asked him.

"I mean," he said slowly, without bothering to look at me, "that it looks like it did when Old Auntie was alive."

"You just told me she's alive. Now you're saying she's dead?"

"No. What I'm saying is Old Auntie's a haunt come back from her grave."

I grabbed Brody's arm and made him stop and look at me. "Do you expect me to believe that?"

He shrugged. "Believe what you like." He turned his back again, but I wasn't through with him.

"This is what I think," I said. "You're dragging me up here to play some kind of trick on me. Which is really awful because my sister is missing and the whole town is looking for her and you're taking advantage of that to get me to go with you. I bet your friends are already up there, getting ready to scare me or something. What kind of kid are you?"

Brody backed away from me. "I'm not up to

anything. I want to help you find your sister, that's all."

We'd reached the steep part of the trail. The trees had thinned out, and the wind was blowing hard enough to knock me over the edge of the hill.

"Ghosts, monsters, places that are ruins in the daytime, but not after dark," I said. "It's all stupid lies, fairy tales. I'm going back to the house. Maybe they've found my sister."

"We're almost there," Brody said. "At least take a look."

I hesitated, stuck between climbing downhill and climbing uphill. I'd come this far, why not go a little farther? What if Erica really was there?

ELEVEN

From the trail, Brody and I climbed down into the hollow. Now that the leaves were gone, the cabin was more visible, but it looked as bad as it had the last time I'd seen it, maybe a little worse.

"Somebody's been here." Brody pointed at Dad's finds—broken stuff, old bottles, animal skulls, still lined up on the stone wall.

"My dad's a photographer. He was taking pictures of those things."

Brody stared at me as if I were even weirder than he'd thought. "You kidding me? Why would anybody take pictures of junk? You got all them beautiful mountains and you waste film on busted plates and broken bottles?"

"Dad's got a digital camera, so he's not wasting film," I said, "and besides, anybody can point a camera at a mountain. My dad's pictures are original. They tell stories."

"Well, let me tell you something. Nobody with any sense messes with Old Auntie's stuff. In fact, hardly anyone ever comes near this place."

"You're here."

"I ain't touched nothing of hers, and I ain't going inside. I'm just trying to help you, that's all."

Brody looked at the cabin's dark doorway. "You went in there, didn't you? That's why the door's open."

A cold wind riffled through the fallen leaves, sending them scurrying through the open door. I shivered, remembering the cabin's dark, damp, creepy atmosphere.

"I didn't stay inside long," I told Brody, "and Erica didn't go in at all. But Dad, well, he poked around, taking pictures, hauling stuff outside, and taking more pictures." I remembered how Erica and I had sat on the wall, barely speaking to each other. Her absence stabbed me with guilt.

Brody kicked at piles of dead leaves and watched then fly up into the air when the wind blew. "Harm's done, I reckon."

"What do you mean? What does all this have to do with my sister?"

He continued to kick at the leaves. "I ain't sure," he said, "but folks say Old Auntie takes a girl and keeps her fifty year—then lets her go and takes another one. It's been going on since folks first came to this place."

I wanted to hit him in his lying mouth. "That's the stupidest thing I've ever heard."

"All I know is, fifty years before Selene disappeared, a girl was took, and one was took fifty years before that."

I sat down on the wall where Erica and I had sat. Brody was an ignorant, superstitious idiot, and I didn't believe a word he said, but I wanted to find my sister, I wanted her to come home, and I wanted us all to go back to Connecticut, to the life we had before we came to this horrible place.

Brody shuffled through the leaves and sat beside me. "Here's what you should do," he said. "Come back here at night. Sneak up real quiet, and don't get too close. The cabin will be like it was two hundred years ago. Old Auntie will be in there, and your sister will be with her."

"How can I believe anything that crazy?"

"'Cause it's the truth." Brody was so close to me I could see his little gray teeth and the dirt rings in his neck. His pale eyes peered out from his tangled hair. "I swear."

The wind died down, as if it were waiting to blow my words across time and into Old Auntie's ears.

"Will you come with me?"

He shook his head and got to his feet. "Let's get out of here."

"Shouldn't we look inside before we go?"

He edged away from the ruins. "Not me," he said. "You go in there, she might take you, too."

"You're afraid," I said.

"So what if I am?" Brody's nose was running. He wiped it on his sleeve, leaving a slimy trail on the suede. "At least I ain't stupid."

"Won't you at least wait outside?"

"Nope." Brody turned away. "I told you what you need to know."

I watched him climb out of the hollow. For a while I heard him on the trail, and then it was just me and the wind and a pair of buzzards circling overhead.

I went to the door of the cabin. "Erica," I called softly. "Erica, are you in there?"

The ruins were silent. The only things moving were the dead vines blowing in the wind and three or four crows cawing to one another from the trees.

I should go home, I thought. *But why?* Everyone except Mom was out searching for my sister.

"Erica," I whispered. "Where are you?"

I heard a muffled noise, as if someone were moving around inside the cabin. What if Erica was trapped there? Not by Old Auntie but by a fallen rafter or something. I walked slowly through the cabin door. *Please please please, let it be my sister, let her be all right.*

It took my eyes a few moments to adjust to the dark. "Erica? Are you in here?"

More noise, frantic sounds, as if someone were trying to hide or run away. "Who's here?" I hoped my voice didn't give away my fear.

Scrabbling sounds. An animal, I thought, a fox or a raccoon.

I started backing toward the door when I saw a flash of green in a shadowy corner, red hair, a blue scarf.

"Erica!" I climbed over a rafter, ducked under a tree that had fallen through the roof, and stumbled across the uneven floor. "Erica, wait! Don't run. It's me, Daniel!"

But she was climbing up a pile of rubble and trying to squeeze through the splintered remains of a window. Frantically, I grabbed her foot and tugged.

"What's wrong with you?" I shouted. "I've come to take you home!"

Suddenly she fell back toward me, and I saw her face. She was not my sister. Sickly and pale, her skin grimy with dirt, she had the look of a wild creature.

I gripped her skinny wrists tightly. "Who are you? How did you get my sister's clothes? Where is she?"

"Let me go, let me go." The girl twisted and turned. She was so thin I was afraid of breaking her bones, but I couldn't let her go, not until she told me where she'd gotten Erica's things.

"That's my sister's jacket, her scarf, her jeans and

sweater, her shoes." I shook her. "Where did you get them?"

"She give 'em to me. Told me they was my clothes, I could keep them."

"Erica gave you her clothes?"

"I don't know nothing about Erica."

"Who gave the clothes to you, then?" I was frantic now. And scared.

"Auntie, she told me to wear 'em home. But I'm scairt to leave the cabin. I don't remember none other home."

She looked around. "Thing is, I don't know what's happened to it. There must have been a fearsome storm to make it look like this."

The girl was beginning to scare me. "What's your name?"

"Let me go." She began to struggle again, but she was weaker now and easier to hold on to.

"Look," I said. "You don't need to be scared. I'm not going to hurt you. Just tell me your name."

"Auntie calls me Girl."

"Girl isn't a name. It's what you are."

"Ain't that what a name is? What you are?"

"No, a name is *who* you are."

"I can't see no difference. Besides, Girl is all the name I got."

She couldn't be who I thought she was. No matter what that liar Brody said, it was impossible — Selene would be almost sixty years old now. Still, I asked anyway. "Does the name Selene Estes mean anything to you?"

"No, no it don't." She struggled to get away. Her wrist bones moved under her skin. "Let me go, please. I didn't do nothing, only what Auntie told me."

Holding her tightly, I pulled her toward the door. "You're coming with me."

"No. No!" She fought me with all her strength, but she was puny and probably underfed.

With one free hand, she grabbed the doorpost and held on. "Let me get the pretty dolly. Auntie give her to me. She said I was to take good care of her."

Keeping her close, I let her go back to the corner where she'd been hiding. There, in a pile of rags, was Little Erica.

Seeing the doll gave me shivers all over. "That's my sister's doll," I said. "She left her in the woods, and someone stole her. Either you or Auntie —"

"I never stole nothing. Auntie found her." The girl picked up the doll by one arm and cuddled her close. "She's the prettiest thing I ever seen. I love her to death."

Little Erica stared at the girl with her blank blue eyes. The small smile still curved the corners of her mouth, but her clothing was soiled, her hair tangled, and her face dirty.

"It's a special doll made to look like my sister," I told the girl.

"Your sister must be real pretty," the girl said.

"Are you sure you haven't seen her? She's been missing since yesterday. Please, you must know something. You have her clothes, her doll."

"I never see anyone but Auntie." The girl looked around, as if she hoped to find Auntie hiding in the shadows. She was as desperate as I was.

"Where is Auntie now?" I asked.

"Gone. She don't want me no more because I can't do the work she needs done. She says she's got someone new to help her."

The girl's eyes filled with tears. I watched them run down her dirty face, leaving little trails in the grime. She was the most pitiful creature I'd ever seen. "Come home with me." I tugged her wrist hard. "You can't stay here all by yourself."

I expected her to fight me, but she followed me outside as if she'd lost all her strength. One hand held Little Erica, the other held mine. Maybe she was as tired of struggling as I was.

She looked back at the cabin so often, she stumbled on roots and stones and almost fell. When she could no longer see the ruin, not even the chimney, she whimpered like a frightened puppy.

"Are you afraid?" I asked her.

"Yes," she whispered. "I'm scairt of leaving the cabin."

"How long have you lived with Auntie?"

"A long, long, long time."

"Were you a baby when you came here?"

"No. I always been just like I am now."

"Then you can't have been with her very long. You'd be older."

The girl looked far off into the trees and the mountains beyond them and up at the sky. "It seems like a long time."

"You know the story about Selene, don't you?"

She shook her head. "I told you and told you, I don't know nothing about Selene."

"Everybody who lives here knows the story!" I yelled at her. "You're just play-acting, aren't you? Did Brody put you up to this?"

"Stop yelling at me. I don't know Brody, and I ain't play-acting."

I studied her pale face, the dark circles under her eyes, the tangled wildness of her red hair. She seemed older than she was—exhausted, malnourished, neglected.

What if Brody was right and this strange girl was Selene? And Old Auntie had swapped her for Erica?

No, I told myself, *no.* Old Auntie was a legend, a folktale, not a real live person. She wasn't out here in the woods, roaming the hills and valleys with Bloody Bones, snatching girls to be her helpers every fifty years. How could anyone believe such nonsense?

Not my parents and not me, either. I held the girl's wrist tighter and made her walk faster. Sooner or later, someone would get the truth out of her.

In Auntie's Cabin

The old woman watches the boy lead Selene away. She chuckles to herself. She can see Selene, but Selene can't see her no more. The boy will take her down the hill to the farm. They'll keep her there until she dies, which won't be long, a few days, a week maybe. It's what happens when they go back to their time. Makes no difference to Auntie. She's got herself a new girl now.

Trouble is, the girl ain't quite up to the work. You'd think she'd never tended a fire or swept a floor or cooked a meal or scrubbed a pot. She acts like she never seen a washtub. She don't know how to make soap or candles or sew a seam. Out in the garden she pulls up more vegetables than weeds. She can't tell an onion from a beet.

She's scairt of spiders and anything else that crawls on floors or scurries across walls or hides in the firewood.

What can Auntie do with such a stupid, lazy girl but scold her and beat her and shut her up in the hidey-hole under the cabin floor.

When she can't stand it no longer, Auntie brings in Bloody Bones and tells the girl he eats bad children like her. The girl cries and shakes with fear at the sight of Auntie's dear boy. He rears up over her, taller than most men. Why, his head bumps the ceiling.

He clacks his teeth and rattles his bones. He makes the girl look into the dark eyeholes in his skull, which is like looking into a bottomless hole, blacker than the blackest night. The girl curls up into a ball like a baby that don't want to be birthed.

After Auntie sends her dear boy outside, the girl tells the old woman she's doing her best, but that ain't good enough, is it? She cries and promises to do better. But she keeps on dropping things and spilling things and breaking things like that's all she's good for.

What Auntie needs is a servant who does everything she's told and never gets tired or needs to be fed. She'd give just about anything to have herself one of them.

She reminds herself she's had the girl for only a few days. Maybe she'll catch on if Auntie beats her harder and locks her up in the hidey-hole more often and threatens to give her to Bloody Bones for his supper.

In the meantime, she better not catch that boy snooping around the cabin again. Or that pitiful Selene either.

TWELVE

When we came in sight of the house, the girl stopped for a moment and stared at it.

"Does it look familiar?" I asked. "Have you ever seen it?"

She shook her head. "I never seen a house that big before. Rich people must live there."

"It's where I live," I told her. "But we're not rich."

She pointed at the junk in the field, which was easier to see now that cold weather had stripped the leaves away. "Look at all the stuff your people threw away. Only rich people would throw out so many good things."

As we drew near the house, the back door flew open and Mom ran toward us. "Erica," she cried. "Thank God you're home! Where have you—"

She stopped a foot away and dropped her outstretched arms. "Who are you?" she said. "Where did you get my daughter's clothes? And her doll?"

Lunging at the girl, Mom grabbed Little Erica out of her arms and clasped the doll to her chest. She looked as if she was about to collapse from disappointment.

The girl reached for Little Erica. "She's mine. Auntie give her to me."

Ignoring the girl, Mom turned to me. "What's the meaning of this? Why have you brought her here? How did she get your sister's things?" Her voice rose with every question, as if she thought I'd played a cruel trick on her.

"She was hiding in the old cabin where Dad took pictures last month," I told Mom. "She says her aunt gave her the clothes and the doll and told her to leave, she was finished with her."

"Oh, no, no, no." Still hugging the doll, Mom sank down on the porch steps. "Erica," she cried. "Erica." She put her head on her knees and sobbed.

"Please." I held the girl's cold little hands. "If you know anything, please tell me."

She darted an ugly look at my mother. "She's got to give my dolly back. Auntie give her to me. She's mine."

Just then the kitchen door opened and a woman stuck her head out. A stranger. "Oh, thank goodness," she said. "You found her."

Mom ran past the woman and disappeared inside, holding the doll and crying. I heard her pound up the back stairs to her room.

The woman stood in the doorway, puzzled. "That's not Erica?" she asked.

I shook my head. "I found her hiding in the old cabin up the trail. She's wearing Erica's clothes, but—"

The woman came down the steps and looked closely at the girl. "What's your name, honey? Where do you live?"

"I'm Girl. I live up yonder with Auntie." She pointed toward the trail that led to the cabin. "Only she don't need me no more. She said so herself. She give me these clothes and told me to go home, but the onliest home I got is with Auntie." She began to cry again, washing more streaks of dirt down her face.

The woman knelt in front of the girl and cupped her face in her hands. "It can't be," she whispered. "God's love, it can't be."

"What can't be, ma'am?" Girl peered at the woman, her face creased in worry.

"Never you mind. It's just my mind wandering." The woman got to her feet and said to me, "You must be Daniel. I'm Mrs. O'Neill. I believe you've already met my husband."

Taking the girl's hand, Mrs. O'Neill said, "Let's take this poor child inside and give her something nice to eat. Hot soup, maybe? She looks cold and hungry."

Mrs. O'Neill led the girl into the kitchen and settled her at the table. While she opened a can of chicken soup with rice and poured it into a pot, the girl looked around.

"My goodness," she said. "You told me you ain't rich, but look at the things you got. Nothing's broken or busted either. It's all clean and new and shiny."

"Well—" How could I tell her that Mom complained about the old-fashioned gas stove she had to light with a match and the refrigerator she had to defrost and the ugly white metal cabinets she hated and the dripping faucets and the black and white squares of cracked linoleum covering the floor?

Mrs. O'Neill made toast and poured two bowls of soup—one for the girl and one for me. Then she sat down with us and studied the girl. The girl's manners were terrible. She slurped and slopped the soup, holding the bowl with one hand, as if she thought I might take it from her. She stuffed the toast into her mouth and almost choked. It was like eating at the table with your dog or something.

When the girl was finished, she wiped her mouth with the back of her hand and blew her nose on the napkin.

Mrs. O'Neill stroked her tangled hair. "How would you like a nice hot bath?"

The girl frowned. "I don't much care for baths."

"Let's go upstairs. When you see the tub, you might change your mind." Mrs. O'Neill led the amazingly docile girl up the back stairs. I waited to hear yelling and screaming and thuds and thumps and doors slamming, but instead, the water ran into the tub and all was quiet.

I fixed a cup of hot chocolate and stood at the kitchen window. The wind was blowing harder now and the short day was running out of light. The second night without Erica was almost here.

After a while Mrs. O'Neill came downstairs carrying the girl. She'd changed her from a scary little wild creature into an almost normal kid. Her hair had been washed and combed, her face and hands were clean, and she was wearing one of Dad's old plaid flannel shirts, last seen hanging on a hook in the bathroom. It fit her like a long nightgown.

"She needs to rest," Mrs. O'Neill said. "I don't want to put her in your sister's room. Can she sleep in your bed for a while?"

I hesitated, but where else was the girl to sleep? At least she was clean now. Reluctantly, I led the way to my room.

By the time Mrs. O'Neill laid her down, the girl was asleep. Covering her with a quilt, she looked at her in the dim light. "You poor child," she whispered. "Where have you been all this time? What's happened to you?"

"Do you think she's Selene?"

"Let her sleep. We'll talk downstairs." Mrs.

O'Neill led me into the hall and closed my bedroom door. Glancing at Mom's closed door, she said, "Don't wake your mother. She's exhausted."

I followed her down the back stairs to the kitchen. Now that it was dark, the wind blew harder. It tugged at the corners of the house and wailed, as if it wanted to come inside. The sound made me cold all over.

"Help me lay out the food," Mrs. O'Neill said. "The men will be back soon, cold and hungry."

Women from town had sent casseroles, sandwich platters, cakes, and pies. It surprised me that they'd cared enough about us, the outsiders, to help. Except for the O'Neills, no one had made any effort to welcome us until now.

While we set out dishes, Mrs. O'Neill said, "We knew Selene Estes, John and I."

"He told me that Selene was best friends with your daughter." I looked at her. "But she'd be almost sixty years old now. And that girl upstairs appears to be my sister's age. How can she be Selene?"

Mrs. O'Neill shook her head. "When I first saw her, I was struck by her resemblance to Selene. It wasn't until I bathed her that I began to think she really is Selene—not only the same hair and the

same eyes, but even the same birthmark on her shoulder."

"Maybe she's faking it," I suggested. "Play-acting a story everybody knows."

"That doesn't explain the birthmark." Mrs. O'Neill paused to set out ladles for the macaroni and the baked beans.

"The trouble is," she went on, "I can't think of any other explanation for your sister's disappearance and this child's appearance."

Maybe I was as crazy as everyone else in this valley, but the more Mrs. O'Neill talked, the more I began to think the girl upstairs might actually be Selene Estes. In this valley, anything could be true, even a conjure woman walking the hills with her pet hog and stealing a girl every fifty years.

"It's happened before, you know," Mrs. O'Neill said. "When Selene disappeared, the search party found a little girl in the woods. Nobody knew who she was, and she couldn't tell them."

"What happened to her?"

Mrs. O'Neill sighed. "They put her in an orphanage. She wouldn't eat or drink. In less than a month, she died without ever saying who she was or where

she came from. But somebody remembered that a child had disappeared fifty years previously. So it seemed the old stories were true after all."

I was about to ask more questions, but the sharp sound of barking dogs scattered my thoughts. I ran to the window. The day had ended and flashlight beams sliced the darkness, illuminating a tree here, a man there. The search party was coming back.

The back door banged open, and Dad led a group of men into the kitchen, big men in work clothes, stomping their feet, red-faced from the cold, talking in low voices.

"Where's your mother?" Dad asked me.

Before I could answer, Mom came stumbling down the back stairs, still half asleep, from the look of her. "Have you found Erica?" She gazed around the room wildly, her eyes flitting from one person to the next. "Where is she?"

The searchers drew together, holding sandwiches but too polite to eat them.

Dad drew Mom close. "I'm so sorry, Martha."

Mom beat her fists against his chest. "You didn't look long enough. You must have missed something, you, you—" She collapsed against him.

He held her up, kept her from falling, stroked her hair, tried to comfort her.

"Believe me, ma'am," Mr. O'Neill told Mom, "we searched every inch of these woods. We didn't find a trace of her. Neither did the dogs."

Mom turned to me. "Where's that girl you brought home? The one with Erica's doll, the one wearing her clothes? Ask *her* where my daughter is. Make her tell you!"

Everyone in the room seemed to stop breathing. No one moved. No one spoke. The only sound was the *tick-tock-tick* of the kitchen clock and the wind rattling the windowpanes.

"What girl?" Dad asked, looking from Mom to me. "What's she talking about, Daniel?"

Before I could answer, Mrs. O'Neill said, "She's talking about Selene. Daniel found her. She's upstairs sleeping."

The group of searchers huddled together, half-finished plates of food in their hands, and mumbled to one another. I heard Selene's name once or twice, but their voices dropped even lower into whispers. Men shook their heads. They looked worried. Frightened, even. A couple of them made excuses and left the house. I heard a car start, saw its headlights, watched its taillights as it sped away.

"What's wrong?" Dad asked Mr. O'Neill. "Why are they leaving?"

"It's the girl," he said slowly, as if answering the question embarrassed him. "They're saying that Old Auntie's got your daughter, and there's no use looking for her."

While Dad stood there, flabbergasted, the last three men thanked us for the food and drink and edged out the back door. In the yard, engines revved, headlights lit the field, and in a couple of minutes the search party was gone.

Mr. O'Neill turned to his wife. "Maybe you should get the girl, bring her down, let Ted see for himself."

Mrs. O'Neill started up the back stairs, and I followed her. Stopping at my closed door, she tapped gently. "So as not to startle her," she whispered.

When no one answered, she opened the door and peeked inside. The window was wide open, and the curtains blew like streamers in the cold air.

Mrs. O'Neill ran to the window and looked out into the night. All that moved were the shadows of trees tossed by the wind.

"She must have gone back to the cabin," I said. "Someone should go after her."

Mrs. O'Neill shook her head. "There's not a man from these parts who'll go near that cabin at night."

"Not even the police?"

"Every one of them grew up here. They've heard stories all their lives about Old Auntie. Most of them swear they've seen her and Bloody Bones in the woods or alongside a dark road."

I watched Mrs. O'Neill hurry down the back stairs, and then I took a quick look around my room. A sweater and pair of jeans I'd left on a chair were gone, and so were my old running shoes. I tiptoed across the hall and checked Mom's room. Little Erica was gone too.

I went to the top of the back stairs and listened. Mom was crying, and Dad was calling the state troopers. "Surely they don't believe in this superstitious nonsense," I heard him say.

Mr. and Mrs. O'Neill were talking in low voices. It sounded as if they were cleaning up the kitchen.

Taking care to make no noise, I crept down the front stairs, grabbed my parka and hat from the coat-rack by the door, and slipped quietly outside. For a second, I hesitated. What if I got lost? I needed someone to come with me, someone who knew the way.

Brody had refused to go near the cabin in broad daylight, but maybe I could talk him into going to the top of the trail with me — it was a long shot, but who else could I ask?

THIRTEEN

By the time I was in sight of Brody's ramshackle old house, I heard a dog bark, then another. In the dim light of the half-moon I saw three or four of them coming down the driveway toward me. What should I do? If I ran, they'd chase me. Maybe if I stood still, they'd just sniff me and leave me alone. They looked like hounds of some kind, not very big, hopefully not very fierce, either.

They stopped about two feet away and kept barking. A light on the front porch came on, and the front door opened.

"Brody!" I yelled. "It's me, Daniel! Call off the dogs."

A gruff male voice called, "You the boy from the Estes farm?"

"Yes, sir." The dogs surrounded me, sniffing and muttering to one another in dog language.

The man whistled, and the dogs ran up the drive toward the house. "Come on," he called to me. "They won't hurt you."

Keeping an eye on the dogs just in case he was wrong, I climbed the porch steps.

"I saw you at the house," he said. "I was in the search party. I'm sorry we didn't find your little sister. We done our best, but—" Shaking his head, he called Brody. "The boy from the Estes farm is here. He wants to see you."

Brody came to the door. "What you want?"

"Can I talk to you about something?" I shot a quick look at his dad, hoping Brody would get the message that this was just between him and me.

"If it's about your sister, I already told you what I think."

"Well, it's actually about Selene."

"Selene?" Mr. Mason leaned closer. I smelled beer and cigarette smoke on his breath. "It's really her, then?"

"The O'Neills think so."

"Where's she now?" Brody asked.

I gave up on trying to keep things between him and me. "I don't know. She ran away."

"Went back to the cabin, I reckon," Mr. Mason said.

"That's what I think." I looked at Brody. "Maybe Erica's there, too. Will you go up there with me?"

Mr. Mason put a hand on my shoulder. "You go on home, boy. Ain't a soul in this valley will go there with you. Certainly not my boy."

"She's my sister," I said. "I have to get her back."

Brody shook his head. "How you think you'll do that? Just knock on the door and say, 'Please, Miss Auntie, give me my sister'?"

Mr. Mason sighed. "Do like I said, boy. Go home. There's nothing you nor me nor anyone else can do for your sister."

"But—"

Mr. Mason stopped me. "Go home. Before you freeze to death."

I left them standing on the porch, watching me, as if to make sure I went home. I walked off in the right direction, but once I reached the end of their driveway, I headed into the woods.

I hadn't gone far when I heard a noise behind me, as if something was following me. I glanced over my shoulder and saw nothing. If I ran, whatever it was would chase me. So I kept walking and hoped it was a fox.

"Wait up, Daniel." Brody ran toward me. He had one of the dogs with him. "You're going up there, ain't you?"

"Are you coming with me?"

"Not me, but I brought Bella. Don't know if she'll protect you, but if you get lost, she'll bring you home." He held out the dog's leash, and I took it.

"She's a good old dog." Brody bent down to scratch behind Bella's ears. "Part beagle, part fox hound, part something bigger—just a mutt, really, but smart as all get-out. You tell her 'home' and she'll lead you there."

"Thanks." I patted Bella, and she wagged her tail. She had a pointed nose, a sharp face, and perked-up ears. Her fur was white with dark patches, and her legs were long. She was sleek and slim, and I could tell by her eyes that she was smart, like Brody said.

"You be careful." Brody stepped back, and I didn't know if he was talking to the dog or to me. "I got to get back before Dad misses me or Bella. He says you're crazy to even think about going near Old Auntie's cabin, but being you're a stranger here, he reckons you're just plain ignorant."

Brody backed away into the woods. "Good luck." With that, he was gone into the night as quickly as he'd come.

Bella looked after him and whined, but she seemed to know she was supposed to stay with me. "Come on, girl," I said, and she darted ahead, as if to lead the way.

I watched her prance along and wished she were mine. It comforted me to think of coming home with Erica and then getting into bed with Bella curled up beside me.

But Bella wasn't mine, and I wasn't sure I'd bring Erica home or even come home myself.

I followed the dog up the trail. Every now and then an owl hooted, sometimes close by, sometimes far away. Once in a while Bella stopped and looked into the woods, as if she saw things invisible to me. She growled or whined, glanced back at me, then went on. She never tugged at the leash but kept a steady pace. She'd been on this path before, I thought, probably hunting raccoons or something.

As the trail grew steeper, Bella paused more often, her body tense. She walked slower, dropping back until she was almost by my side. The wind blew harder up there, and the moon slid in and out from the clouds, sometimes lighting the path, sometimes casting it into darkness. I shivered; my teeth chattered—not just because I was cold, which I was, but also because we'd reached the drop-off.

Bella pressed against my side, and I felt her body tremble. "Careful, girl," I whispered. "We're right on the edge of the trail."

From where I stood, I looked down, way down into the valley, which was awash with moonlight. One misstep, and you'd be over the side of the hill, falling, falling, falling to certain death on the rocks below.

Staying as far away from the edge as possible, I forced myself to keep climbing. Finally we reached the top. The hollow lay in shadows, darker than any-where else, as black as an underground cavern.

Suddenly Bella stiffened and moved forward, ears erect, body tense, growling softly. Something moved in the hollow below us.

Bella's growl turned to a whine, and she pressed against me as if she were frightened.

For a second, I hoped I'd found Erica, but in-stead Selene stepped out of the cabin's shadow, more woebegone than ever.

Bella whined and looked up at me. "It's okay," I whispered to the dog.

Selene stayed where she was. "Will that dog bite me?"

I shook my head. "She's a good dog. Her name's Bella."

As Selene came closer, Bella made no effort to greet her. If anything, she pressed closer to me. She was still trembling.

Selene looked at the dog. "She don't like me," she said sadly.

I wasn't interested in how Bella felt about Se-lene. All I wanted was to find my sister. "You said the cabin would look like it did when you lived here."

"It does," Selene said. "Can't you see the light in the window?"

I peered into the blackness. "There's nothing there," I said.

She pointed. "Right there. And smoke's coming from the chimney. Your sister's in there. I seen her through the window, but I can't get in."

I stared into the darkness until my eyeballs ached, but I couldn't see anything. "Are you telling the truth or play-acting?"

"I'm telling you the honest-to-God truth. She's setting by the fire, stirring the pot like I used to. Only she's not doing it right, and Auntie will give her a walloping when she comes home."

"She'll beat my sister?"

"That's what she does if you don't do things right—she wallops you. I used to get bruises all over me till I learned."

Nobody was going to hurt my sister. If she was in that cabin, I'd break the door down and rescue her. With Bella and Selene behind me, I plunged downhill into the hollow, scrambling and slipping on loose stones. But all I saw were the same ruins I'd always seen.

Bella hung back, as if she knew something was in the ruins, but Selene ran to one of the few standing walls and looked through a broken window.

"There she be, your sister, just like I said. I don't see my auntie, though. She must be out in the woods."

I watched Selene struggle to open the sagging door. "Let me in, girl!" She pounded on the wood with her fists. "Let me in!"

I pulled her away. "There's nothing here. You're imagining it."

Bella whined and danced around me, but I was too busy with Selene to pay any attention to the dog. Finally the dog grabbed my parka. Frantic with fear, she tugged and growled through her clenched teeth and did her best to drag me away from the cabin's ruins.

In the struggle, I lost my grip on Selene, and she ran into the woods, calling for Auntie.

Even with the girl gone, Bella wouldn't let go of my parka. She continued to whine and growl and pull me toward the trail.

Freeing myself from Bella, I chased Selene. The dog darted in front of me and blocked my way. I dodged and shouted Selene's name until I was hoarse. She was gone. I'd lost her, just as I'd lost Erica.

At least that's what I thought, until Bella cowered beside me. The woods were very still. The wind stopped. The moon hid behind the clouds.

Coming toward us was Selene. An old woman walked beside her. She leaned on a staff and carried a bundle. Her long skirt was the color of the winter sky on a starless night, her shawl as black as midnight. Long strands of white hair blew about her head. Shadows hid her face.

I wanted to run, but I couldn't move. Neither could Bella. We were frozen, paralyzed, under a spell. We could do nothing but watch the two of them approach. Old Auntie shoved Selene toward me. "I brung her back. She ain't mine no more. Take her home and keep her there, boy. She's your sister now. The girl in the cabin is my girl. Look for her in fifty years if you want her back."

"No, Auntie," Selene cried. "Ain't I worked hard all my life for you? Give her back and let me stay with you. I'll work hard, I'll do better, I promise you."

Selene tried to embrace Old Auntie, but the old

woman pushed her away. The girl sprawled on the ground at my feet. Bella sniffed her and whimpered.

"Now, you go on and get out of here," Old Auntie told her. "Don't let me see you no more. Don't come looking for me. Stay away from my cabin. You hear me?"

Selene lay on the ground, a pathetic little creature. Her body shook with sobs.

"If you come begging at my door again, I'll send my boy after you." Old Auntie spit on the ground. "You know what he can do, Girl. He'll make you sorry. And that's the truth."

Selene shuddered and peered into the darkness. "Is he close by?" she whispered.

"Bloody Bones can be here or he can be far, but I reckon he's close enough to come if I whistle." She leaned down to peer into Selene's face. "You want me to fetch him?"

"No, no, Auntie, don't whistle for him," Selene begged. "I'll go away and I won't come back no more." While she spoke, she stared about wild-eyed, searching the darkest shadows, as if Bloody Bones might be hiding behind a tree or a bush or a rock.

The moon came out then and shone full on

Auntie's face. Her eyes were sunk deep in their sockets, her skin stretched tight across her skull. A few yellow teeth sat crooked in her lipless mouth and her nose was no more than sharp bone. She looked like she should be in her grave, not here in the woods.

She screeched with laughter and stuck her face so close to mine that I could smell her breath, rotten with decay. "Why, boy, I believe you ain't never seen the likes of me afore."

I backed away, stumbled over Bella, and fell flat. The dog whined and cowered beside me. Behind the old conjure woman, I saw something move in the woods, snapping branches under its feet, snuffling, rooting in the dead leaves.

Auntie laughed again, a wild whoop this time that echoed from tree to tree and bounced off rocks. "He's here," she hissed to Selene. "Old Bloody Bones hisself. Get yourselves away from here afore I send him after you both — and the dog, too."

In a swirl of skirt and shawl, Auntie turned her back and strode away. The wind picked up, the woods stirred. She was gone.

But instead of following her, Bloody Bones stepped out of the woods and into the moonlight.

His head was a hog's skull, the rest of him bones. Taller than my father, he walked toward us on two feet. His ragged overalls fluttered about him as he raised his arms to show us the bear claws. Then he grinned to show us the panther's teeth. As he moved slowly toward us, a whistle sounded in the trees. His head swung toward the sound, and he snorted.

"Come to me, dear boy," Old Auntie called from somewhere in the woods. "Let them go for now, but if they come back, eat them."

With a grunt of disappointment, Bloody Bones turned away and lumbered into the dark.

Bella threw back her head and howled, the eeriest sound I'd ever heard a dog make. Turning to Selene, who still lay on the ground sobbing, the dog sniffed her cautiously, going over every inch of her, as if reading the fine print in a contract. Then, looking up at me, she licked the girl's cheek.

My heart pounded and my knees shook with fear, but I leaned over Selene. "You heard what she said," I told her. "We have to get out of here."

With Bella leading the way, Selene stumbled silently beside me, keeping a tight grip on the doll. When we got to the hollow, she looked at me. "I can't see the cabin no more," she said. "The lights are out and the chimney smoke's gone."

She ran to the broken window and peered inside. She seemed to see what I saw—a ruined cabin rotting away in the woods, full of shadows, dark and abandoned.

"Come on." I held out my hand. "There's nothing here for you or me now."

In Auntie's Cabin Again

The old woman comes into the cabin and slams the door behind her. Her shadow rises up and rolls across the room before her. She's so angry, she slaps the girl across the face, hard enough to knock her out of the chair where she's been sleeping.

The girl cringes on the floor, covering her face with her hands. "Don't hit me no more, Auntie," she begs. "I ain't been sleeping long."

But the old woman picks up her stick and whacks the girl on the back. "Look there – you done let the fire go out! Cain't I trust you to do nothing right?"

The girl scrambles to her feet and tries to light the

fire, but she's fumble-fingered with fear. Any minute Auntie will hit her again.

"Get out of my way." The old woman shoves the girl aside and squats to light the fire. She hears Selene crying outside, hears the boy dragging her away.

"Your brother come here to get you," she tells the girl. "But me and my dear boy chased him off. Don't make no difference. He's got hisself another sister now."

The girl stares at her, blank eyed. She doesn't have a brother. She's Auntie's girl. She's been here all her life. Just her and Auntie. Nobody else. Nobody except — except — her eyes go to the window. The pale face of Auntie's dear boy peers in at her. He grins and shows her his sharp teeth. But he's not her brother. Or is he? She doesn't know. She doesn't know anything.

The old woman sinks into her rocking chair and laughs at the girl's mystified face. "You ain't got no idea what I'm talking about, do you?" She feels like hitting her again. Or kicking her. Or throwing something at her. But she's tired from walking in the woods.

She leans toward the girl, baring her yellow teeth in a smile as hideous as the dear boy's wicked grin. "Your brother won't be back," she says. "My dear boy has scairt him off. But if'n he does come back, you won't go with him 'cause you love your old auntie and you know she loves you."

She reaches out and pinches the girl's cheek. "Say you love me. Tell me, let me hear you."

Tears of pain fill the girl's eyes. "I love you so much, Auntie, more than anything." She wants to pull away from those fingers and their sharp nails, but if she does, Auntie will pinch harder.

"Tell me I'm good to you. Tell me I give you what you deserve."

"You're good to me, Auntie," she whispers. "You give me what I deserve."

The old woman releases her grip on the girl's cheek and settles back in her rocking chair. The fire flickers and casts dancing shadows on the walls and across the ceiling.

The girl crouches by the hearth. Over her head, three bats hang upside down, sleeping the winter away. Bundles of dry herbs dangle from the rafters. The girl hates their smell. The whole cabin reeks of deadly nightshade, henbane, hemlock, and foxglove – poisons, every one of them. Auntie makes potions from them, things that harm and hurt and sometimes kill.

She tells the girl about them and cackles. "I got me a bunch of names on a list, both the living and the dead. One by one I gets my revenge on them who done wrong to me."

In dark corners, black widows and other poisonous spiders lurk. The girl is afraid to sweep away their webs. She's also afraid of the scuttling noises the rats make. Sometimes she glimpses them darting across the floor from one corner to another. They're bigger than cats, and their teeth are long and sharp.

But most of all she's afraid of Bloody Bones. If she dared, she'd give him one of those little bottles of poison and kill him dead. That's how much she hates Auntie's dear boy.

But she doesn't hate Auntie. Oh, no. She loves Auntie. Auntie is all she has to keep her safe from Bloody Bones.

FOURTEEN

Bella led us eagerly down the path, never faltering, steering us deftly around rocks and roots and fallen branches. I'd lost the flashlight in the confusion and was grateful for the dog's sure footing.

All the way down Brewster's Hill, neither Selene nor I said one word. We didn't look behind us, for fear of what might be following us. Every noise made my heart pound. I thought I heard Bloody Bones snuffle, heard his hooves on the stones, smelled his hot, bloody breath, thought he was getting closer, closer. Soon he'd have us both, and Bella, too.

But when we came out of the woods at the bottom of Brewster's Hill, Bloody Bones was not behind us after all. Or if he had been, he wasn't there then. I paused and took a deep breath. Here on the edge of the field, with the house in sight, I felt almost safe. Bella licked my hand and wagged her tail. I watched her trot off toward Brody's house, sad to see her leave.

Selene's cold hand touched mine. She'd been crying silently. "I got no one now," she whispered. Her voice was like a song you hear in the dark just before you fall asleep.

I squeezed her hand and felt its tiny bones shift in my grip. People were so fragile, so easily broken, so hard to put back together. "Mr. and Mrs. O'Neill will take care of you," I told her.

Selene said nothing, but she let me lead her across the field toward the farmhouse.

The back porch light lit the yard like a spotlight. Before I opened the door, Dad threw it wide. "Where have you been?" he shouted. "Aren't we worried enough without your going off somewhere without a word to anybody?"

His eyes lit on Selene. "Is this the girl your mother was talking about?"

I nodded and squeezed Selene's cold hand. "She ran away, and I went to find her."

Mom came into the kitchen, followed by the O'Neills. Looking at Selene with hostility, Mom said, "She took the doll with her. And she's wearing your clothes, Daniel."

"Now, Martha." Mrs. O'Neill patted Mom's shoulder in an effort to calm her. "What have I been telling you?"

"Nothing I believe." Mom never took her eyes off Selene. "What's your name?"

"Girl." Selene lowered her head. She was so pale and so little and so skinny—how could Mom be so mean to her?

Mom scowled down at Selene. "Your real name. Tell me your *real* name. Tell me who you are."

"I'm his sister now."

Mom seemed too stunned to speak, but Dad said, "You are not my son's sister!"

"That's what Auntie said," Selene whispered. "I'm to be his sister now. To take the place of the other."

Before Mom or Dad could say more, Mr. O'Neill knelt beside Selene and studied her face. "I knew you a long time ago, Selene. You lived right here in this house. You were friends with my daughter Eleanor. I knew your parents, too. Do you remember my wife and me?"

"I never lived here," Selene told Mr. O'Neill, obviously confused. "I don't have no mama or daddy. No friends, either. I've lived my whole life long with Auntie. But she don't want me anymore."

Pointing at me, she added, "Auntie says I'm to be *his* sister now. And I'll be hurt bad if I come back to the cabin looking to be with her again."

"I can't take this anymore." Mom left the kitchen and clattered up the back stairs. We all heard her bedroom door slam shut. It was just like before, only this time she didn't take the doll.

"Will you please tell me what's going on, Daniel?" Dad asked.

I did my best to explain it, but I knew I was losing him. He kept interrupting and saying, "This is ridiculous. Do you expect me to believe you?"

Mr. O'Neill sighed. "I tried to tell you, Ted."

Dad turned his back and followed Mom upstairs. The O'Neills, Selene, and I were left in the kitchen. I had no idea what to say or do.

Mrs. O'Neill sat down and lifted Selene into her lap. The girl leaned against Mrs. O'Neill and pressed her face against the woman's body. Little Erica stared over her shoulder, her blank blue eyes focused on nothing.

"Do you remember anything about this house?" Mrs. O'Neill asked Selene. "Your mama or your daddy?"

Selene shook her head. "I been tellin' you and tellin' you. I'm Auntie's girl."

"But not anymore," Mrs. O'Neill said.

Selene didn't say anything.

"She's almost asleep, poor thing," Mr. O'Neill murmured.

"How about we take her to our house?" Mrs. O'Neill asked me, as if she expected me to make the decision. "The very sight of her upsets your mother and angers your father."

"Maybe that would be best," I said.

I found a spare blanket and gave it to Mr. O'Neill. He wrapped it around Selene and carried her out to the car.

I stood on the back porch, shivering in the cold.

"Just make sure she doesn't run off," I called. "She'd freeze to death in those woods."

"Don't worry," Mr. O'Neill said. "We'll keep her safe."

"Come by and see us tomorrow," Mrs. O'Neill added. "I've got things to talk about with you."

I watched the car turn and head down the driveway. When its taillights disappeared around a curve, I went back inside. I was so tired—so, so tired. So sad. My head ached, as if my brain were about to explode from trying to understand what I'd seen in the woods. It couldn't be true. It was true. It couldn't be. It was.

The next morning, I woke up early, ate breakfast, and left a note telling Mom and Dad I was at the O'Neills' house. It was cold, and the sky was a solid light gray, so heavy with clouds that the sun couldn't break through. It felt as if snow was coming. Maybe it was better to think of Erica being with Old Auntie than to imagine her wandering in the woods, lost and cold and hungry.

I saw Brody at the end of our driveway. He was

wearing his suede jacket and a pair of filthy pink tennis shoes with holes in the toes.

Bella was with him, trotting along the edge of the road and sniffing in the weeds. When she saw me, she ran up and wagged her tail.

"Did you go to the cabin?" Brody asked. "Was Selene there?"

I looked up from petting Bella and nodded. "She swore Erica was inside, but all I saw were ruins, looking just like they always have."

"Did you see Old Auntie?"

"I was never so scared in my whole life. She's, she's—" I couldn't say any more for fear of somehow bringing her to me.

Wiping his nose on the sleeve of his jacket, Brody stared at me. "What did she do? What did she say?"

"She told me to take Selene home. She said she's my sister now."

"That girl don't want to be your sister." Brody spat on the ground.

"She wants to be with Auntie, but Auntie says that if Selene comes near the cabin, she'll sic Bloody Bones on her."

Brody's eyes widened. "Did you see him?"

I stared off into the woods and tried not to think about what I'd seen. "He's horrible, just like you said."

"Did he chase you?"

"No. He stood there and looked at us, and then Old Auntie whistled for him."

Brody sucked in his cheeks and let his breath out in a puff of air. "You must be really brave or really stupid, I'm not sure which, but I'm glad you brung my dog home safe."

With Bella between us, we stood on the edge of the road for a while, staring at the trees, as if we expected to see Bloody Bones or Old Auntie. A red-tailed hawk soared overhead, dark against the pale sky, and the wind picked up. It looked more like snow than ever. You could practically smell it in the wind.

"Is Selene at your house?" Brody asked.

I shook my head. "The O'Neills took her home with them last night. That's where I'm going."

"Can I come with you? I want to see that girl."

He and I and the dog walked on down the road. Snow began falling. Bella snapped at the flakes, and Brody opened his mouth like a kid and caught snow on his tongue. Even though I was half crazy with worry about my sister, I did the same. I've always loved the way snow feels on my tongue.

When we got to the O'Neills' house, the snow was at least half an inch deep, falling fast and thick now, making it hard to see. Trees blurred, fields blended in with the sky, and the house was no more than a faint outline against the smudge of woods behind it.

Mrs. O'Neill opened the door wide and let us all in, even Bella, who immediately made herself at home in front of the fire. "You must be freezing," she said.

Brody stopped in the living room doorway and stared at Selene, who was sitting on a couch beside Mr. O'Neill. A photo album lay open in his lap, but she seemed more interested in combing Little Erica's hair than in looking at the pictures. She didn't appear to notice the dog, Brody, or me.

"Get those wet shoes off, boys, and dry your feet by the fire," Mr. O'Neill said. "How's your father doing, Brody?"

"'Bout the same." Brody busied himself taking off his shoes and laying them carefully on the hearth.

He'd already shed his jacket and hung it on the back of a wooden chair in the corner. "He ain't found a job yet."

I put my hiking boots beside his worn-out tennis shoes. It always makes me feel guilty to have better stuff than other people. Something's wrong with a world that lets me have waterproof boots and someone else have tennis shoes with holes in the toes.

I looked at Selene, but she kept her eyes on the doll. Mr. O'Neill nudged her. "Aren't you going to say hello to Daniel? You haven't met Brody before — he lives on the other side of your old home, just over the bridge."

Without looking at either one of us, she shook her head. She wore a gray plaid dress and a dark green sweater. Her hair had been combed until it was free of tangles. If you didn't look too closely, you'd think Selene was a perfectly normal girl. Maybe a little shy, but nothing out of the ordinary.

When she finally raised her head and stared at us with those pale green eyes, you could see right away that she was different, not normal after all, a wild child with wild ways.

Brody actually took a step back when he saw Selene's pale, pointed face and her fierce eyes. For a moment I thought he was going to grab his jacket and shoes and leave, but he stayed where he was, wiping his nose and staring at the girl.

Ignoring Brody's reaction to Selene, Mr. O'Neill motioned to us to join him. "I'm showing Selene some pictures. Maybe you'd like to see them too."

I sat beside him, on the opposite side from Selene. Brody perched next to me on the arm of the sofa, ready to head for home if he needed to. He was a little wild himself, but nothing like Selene.

"This is my daughter's first-grade class picture." Mr. O'Neill pointed at a tall dark-haired girl in the back row of a faded black-and-white print. "That's Eleanor." Glancing at Selene, he moved his finger slowly to a child sitting in the middle of the front row. "And this is Selene."

Selene faced the camera, a big grin on her face. Like the other girls, she wore a dress with a round collar, very much like the one she was wearing now. Her curly red hair touched her shoulders.

Brody leaned past me to see. "It's her all right."

We both looked at Selene. With her face turned away from the photo album, she continued to comb Little Erica's hair.

"Selene disappeared not long after that picture was taken," Mr. O'Neill went on. "I've been showing her photos taken here at our house."

I looked at a page of snapshots of Selene and Eleanor. It was hard to believe that the frightened, unhappy kid sitting with us on the sofa had once hung upside down by her knees from a tree limb, ridden a bike, splashed in a swimming pool, and made silly faces.

"This is Selene's mother." Mr. O'Neill pointed to a pretty woman pulling both girls on a sled on a snowy day and smiling at the camera. "And her father. See? That's Selene on her dad's shoulders. She must have been two or three."

Mrs. O'Neill joined us then. "Don't you want to look at the pictures, Selene?" she asked gently. "It might help you remember your family—and who you are."

Keeping her head down, Selene said, "I know who I am."

"These were taken at Eleanor's seventh birthday party." Mr. O'Neill turned the page and moved the album closer to Selene, but she slid off the sofa and sat in a rocking chair by the fire.

Mrs. O'Neill smiled. "It was November, but unseasonably warm, so the children played outside. Look, here's Selene. I still remember that pretty blue dress—she was so adorable. And so happy." She paused a moment and turned to Brody. "Look at this—it's your uncle Silas."

Brody leaned closer to stare at the skinny boy in the photo. "Whew, he sure don't look like that now—bald and fat. Got a scruffy old beard and spends most of his time down at the tavern on State Street."

"Here's your dad. See? Right there beside Silas."

Brody squinted at the slightly blurry face of a five-year-old. "Now, he ain't changed so much, except for his hair, which is mostly gone. He's still skinny as a fence post."

Mrs. O'Neill's eyes returned to Selene in her blue dress. She was backlit by the sun, and her hair glowed in its light. "A week after the party, Selene disappeared," she told us. "Eleanor cried for weeks.

She's never forgotten Selene or gotten over her disappearance."

We all looked at the girl across the room. Humming to herself, she rocked the doll. She might as well have been alone, for all the attention she paid us.

Mr. O'Neill closed the album and laid it gently on the table. "I was hoping," he said wearily, "that seeing the pictures might make her remember, but I guess not."

He excused himself, saying he had work to do in his shop. "I'm building a dollhouse for my granddaughter—still hoping to finish it in time for her birthday. Maybe I'll build the next one for Selene."

Mrs. O'Neill beckoned to Brody and me. "You boys, come along with me."

We followed her down a narrow hall to the kitchen. It was big and modern, the kind of place Mom wanted so badly. I looked through a sliding glass door to an outside deck. The snow was about an inch and a half deep on the railing and still falling. The mountains had vanished behind a white curtain, and the woods were hard to see. Erica was out there somewhere.

"I told you last night I wanted to talk to you, Daniel," Mrs. O'Neill said. "You, too, Brody."

She sat on a stool at the counter, and we perched on either side of her. "First of all," she said, "I've called Eleanor and told her the news. If the snow doesn't keep her from coming, she'll be here one day this week. Maybe, just maybe, she'll find a way to communicate with Selene."

"But what about Erica?" I asked. "Now that we know where she is, can we get her back?"

Turning to Brody, Mrs. O'Neill asked him what he knew about an old woman who lived down at the end of Railroad Avenue.

"Miss Perkins?" Brody hunched his shoulders. "She's crazy, that's what. Nobody has nothing to do with her unless it's something secret, like, like — well, I don't exactly know what — except every cat and dog that goes missing ends up in her stew pot. And maybe other things, too."

"Yes, I've heard plenty of stories myself." Mrs. O'Neill paused. "But I've also heard she's a descendant of Old Auntie and knows a thing or two about conjuring herself."

Brody folded his arms across his skinny chest, hiding the puppy face that was knitted into the moth-eaten sweater he wore. "Not to be rude or nothing, but I ain't going near that old lady. And you shouldn't either."

Mrs. O'Neill turned to me. "How about you, Daniel?"

What choice did I have? If I refused, it would be like saying I didn't care what happened to my sister. "As long as somebody comes with me," I said. "I'll go."

I heard a whisper of sound behind me and turned to see Selene standing in the doorway. "Can I come too?"

"Oh, no, Selene," Mrs. O'Neill said. "This woman—"

"I heard you say she's kin to Auntie. Maybe she can change me for that other girl, the new one she got to help her. Then everybody'd be happy. They all want the new one back, and no one wants me."

Mrs. O'Neill studied the girl's pale face. "Oh, Selene, that's not true. Of course we want Erica back, but we don't want to lose you."

"You got to take me to see her, you got to!" Se-lene cried. "She's my onliest chance to see Auntie again."

"Maybe you should be there," Mrs. O'Neill said slowly. "Maybe Miss Perkins should see you."

Selene leaned against the doorframe. Holding the doll tightly, she hummed to herself. It was the same tune I'd heard Erica hum, a strange, sad song, like an old ballad, but without words.

I turned away from the girl's sad face. Sometimes I couldn't bear to look at her. What if my sister came back in fifty years, looking just like Selene?

"When should we go see Miss Perkins?" I asked Mrs. O'Neill.

She went to the sliding doors and peered out. "The snow's letting up," she said. "If the roads are plowed tonight, we can go to Woodville tomorrow."

She was right. I could see the mountains again, as soft against the sky as clouds resting on earth. The trunks of trees in the woods were smudged charcoal lines on white paper.

"I ain't going with you," Brody said, "so don't bother to ask."

Nobody argued with him. It was bad enough that Selene was coming. We didn't need Brody, too.

He joined Mrs. O'Neill at the door and pressed his nose against the glass, making a big smear. "Bella and me should get on home soon." He didn't make a move to get his jacket or the dog, but stood watching the snow.

"Let me give you lunch first. How about grilled cheese sandwiches and hot chocolate?"

While Mrs. O'Neill fixed the sandwiches, Selene stood at the window, her back to us. From the way she held Little Erica up to the glass, I guessed she was showing her the snow.

Mrs. O'Neill set sandwiches and hot chocolate on the counter and called Selene.

"I don't want to eat with them boys." She didn't turn around, but stayed at the window, her back to the room.

"Well, how about if I seat you at the breakfast table over by the window?"

Selene agreed to that, but made sure her chair faced the window, not us.

After we'd eaten, Brody thanked Mrs. O'Neill

for lunch. "I really ought to go home before my daddy starts in to worrying about me."

I said goodbye to the O'Neills and followed Brody outside. There must have been six inches of snow on the ground, and it was still falling. Bella leaped and danced ahead of us, barking as if the snow were the best thing she'd ever seen. My father always said it didn't take much to make a dog happy. Bella was certainly proof of that.

FIFTEEN

I let myself into the house quietly. No fire in the living room, no smell of cooking, but I heard low voices in the kitchen. Mom and Dad were sitting at the table, their breakfast dishes pushed to one side. Last night's pots and pans and dishes filled the sink.

Caught by surprise, they looked at me as if I were a stranger. "Daniel," Dad said. "We thought you'd stay overnight with the O'Neills. The snow and all—" He waved a hand vaguely at the window.

"It's almost stopped."

Mom turned her attention from me to her coffee. I'd never seen her look so bad. Her hair was limp and uncombed, her face shadowed with grief. She wore an old UMass sweatshirt and baggy corduroy pants, the same clothes she'd worn since Erica disappeared.

Dad hadn't shaved, and gray stubble covered his cheeks. His eyes were puffy and red rimmed. He wore a navy sweatshirt and sweatpants, an outfit he usually reserved for watching TV after dinner.

There was an empty wine bottle on the table and an ashtray full of cigarette butts and ashes.

"What's going on?" I asked, fearful that something bad had happened—they'd found Erica dead in the snow or frozen in the woods or, or . . .

"Nothing," Dad said. "Nothing is going on. Nothing has changed. She's still missing, and no one wants to look for her in this snow."

"They don't want to look for her at all," Mom said. "Even the state police say it's hopeless." She lit a cigarette and inhaled so deeply that she coughed.

"Please don't smoke," Dad said. "You know I hate it."

"I'll smoke if I want to." She gave him a nasty look. "It calms my nerves."

Dad shoved his chair away from the table and started up the back stairs.

"Where are you going, Ted?" Mom called.

"To check my email. Just in case—"

"Just in case what?"

"Just in case . . ." He didn't finish the sentence.

"Face it, we'll never see her again." Mom started crying.

Dad went to his den and slammed the door.

My parents had lost their minds. Their marriage was collapsing. The only way to fix things was to find Erica and bring her home. And no one could do that except me.

The next day was gray and cloudy, and the snow was pockmarked with drops falling from trees. School wasn't closed, but Mom said she didn't want me going back yet. That was fine with me.

"The kids and the teachers will torment you with questions," she said. "I don't want them making you even more miserable. People are so insensitive at times like this."

"Is it okay if I go to Woodville with Mrs. O'Neill?

She knows someone who might be able to help Selene."

Mom shrugged. "Go ahead, do what you want, but please tell Mrs. O'Neill I want Erica's doll returned."

Her voice sounded mean and hard again. The mother I used to know had disappeared with Erica.

Mom went to the kitchen and stood at the window, smoking and watching the woods, as if she were waiting to see Erica run toward the house. Dad was working at his computer. He'd set up a website in hope of getting in touch with someone who'd seen Erica. He had lots of hits, all worthless. A man had seen her in a diner in Kentucky; a woman had seen her in a Walmart in Tennessee. Someone else saw her waving frantically from the rear window of a car on I-95 North. She was in Alaska, Italy, California. On buses, planes, trains. Those who hadn't seen her either prayed for her or accused my father of faking the disappearance. Maybe he'd murdered her. Maybe he wanted money. Yet Dad checked every one of them and alerted the police when he received a sighting.

With no one to talk to and nothing to do, I spent most of the day in my room, playing games on my iPad to keep from blaming myself over and over again for Erica's disappearance. Why hadn't I let her pick up the doll? Why? Why?

The phone rang around two. It was Mrs. O'Neill. She'd come by for me in half an hour, if that was okay with my parents. I told her it was fine. I didn't say they probably wouldn't even notice I was gone.

When Mrs. O'Neill arrived, she handed me the clothes Selene had helped herself to. I left them on the porch so I wouldn't have to go back inside, where my parents were arguing endlessly over whose fault it was.

I sat in the front seat, and Selene sat in the back. I guessed she was wearing clothes Eleanor had worn when she was little—a blue jacket with a belt and a fake fur collar, corduroy jeans, and a pair of yellow rubber boots. Selene didn't look at me, but kept her head bent over the doll. Nothing unusual about that.

Railroad Avenue was in the worst part of Woodville. We passed taverns, boarded-up stores, an abandoned gas station. A stray dog poked its nose into overflowing garbage cans that were half buried in snow. Newspapers blew down the icy sidewalks. A few people came in and out of a shabby market.

Mrs. O'Neill drove slowly, looking for the house number. "Forty-eight eleven," she said. "This is it."

She parked in front of a shabby little house that was badly in need of paint. The roof sagged under the weight of the snow. No one had shoveled the walk. No footprints led to the door.

"Do you think she's home?" I asked.

"Let's find out." Mrs. O'Neill picked up Selene and led the way to the porch through knee-deep snow.

Not a sound from inside. She pressed the bell, waited awhile, and tried again.

"Maybe it's broken," I said.

She nodded and knocked. Once, twice, several times. I shivered from cold and maybe a little fear. The house was rundown and dark. One window was covered with a sheet of plastic, another boarded up. The porch buckled under our feet. The walls were sprayed with gang tags and badly drawn pictures of witches and devils and monsters.

Just as we were about to give up, the door opened a crack and a woman peered out. She was not just old—she was ancient. Bent and bony, no bigger than Selene, her flyaway white hair floated around her head like dandelions gone to seed. She'd wrapped herself in a thick knitted shawl of every imaginable color woven into complex patterns—a sun here, a moon there, stars all over, rivers and trees and birds and animals. A person could look at it all day and still find something he hadn't noticed before.

"What do you want with me?" she croaked. Her eyes glittered in her shadowy face.

Mrs. O'Neill put Selene down and held out her hand. "I'm Irene O'Neill, and I've come to you for help." The old woman looked at her hand, but didn't take it.

"I don't help strangers." She was about to slam the door in our faces.

"Wait, don't be so hasty!" Mrs. O'Neill pushed Selene forward. "What if I told you this girl is Selene Estes? Would you help us then?"

Miss Perkins froze. Instead of slamming the door, she leaned out and peered down at Selene, studying her as if she were a book she needed to learn. She touched Selene's cheek, stared into her eyes, examined a strand of her hair. I think she even sniffed her. Shaking her head, she mumbled and muttered to herself and gazed over Selene's head at the darkening sky.

At last she spoke to Mrs. O'Neill. "I smell Auntie on this here girl. I feel her touch."

Selene tugged at Miss Perkins's arm. "Can you make her take me back, ma'am? I'm still strong. I can do the work."

"Go back to Auntie? Whatever for?"

"She told me to go live someplace else, she was done with me. But I ain't done with her."

When Selene began to sob, Mrs. O'Neill tried to comfort her, but the girl pulled away. "Leave me be," she cried. "I don't want nobody but Auntie!"

"I reckon you better come inside." Miss Perkins opened the door wide, and we followed her into a dark hallway. The house smelled of mildew and mold and cat pee. An old carpet, stained and worn through in spots, covered the floor. Bulging boxes and bundles stood in piles and stacks against the walls. It was a good thing Miss Perkins was a skinny little woman. A normal-size person would need to turn sideways to squeeze down that hall.

At the top of a flight of steps, several cats stared down at us. Others crouched on the stacks of boxes. A few more wound around our ankles, meowing.

To our left, raggedy velvet curtains framed a

doorway into a small room that was also filled with bundles and boxes, with just enough space left for a sagging couch and a rocking chair. The windows were covered with blinds. A small fire burned on the hearth, barely enough to light the room, even though it wasn't much past three o'clock.

"Set there on the sofa," Miss Perkins said as she took a seat in the rocking chair.

Displacing more cats, the three of us crowded onto the sofa, Selene on one side of Mrs. O'Neill and me on the other. Pressed close to her, I felt the tension in her body. I was tense too. Scared, even. The house reeked of dark secrets, of sorrow and misery. I understood why Brody had refused to come with us.

I glanced at Selene. She hadn't stopped staring at Miss Perkins. Maybe not even to blink. She and the doll had the same blank-eyed look on their faces.

"Now then," Miss Perkins said to Mrs. O'Neill. "Here's the way I see it. Auntie must have took the boy's sister when she let Selene go. She'll work his sister fifty years, and then, when she's worn-out like this one, she'll let her go and take another girl."

"I ain't worn-out. I can still do the work," Selene insisted.

Miss Perkins ignored Selene. Closing her eyes, she rocked in her chair for a few moments, nodding to herself, clasping and unclasping her hands. "You won't like it, but here's the truth of it," she said. "Auntie's been doing this for over two hundred years now. She's got no reason to quit, and I ain't got the power to stop her."

I peered into the old woman's face. Her eyes, hidden by drooping lids and wrinkles, were set way back in her skull, so I couldn't guess what she was thinking or even be sure where she was looking.

"Please," I whispered. "There must be something you can do to get Erica back. My parents are going crazy."

Firelight danced across her face, making her wrinkles stand out as if they'd been carved into her skin. "What on earth do you want me to do, boy?"

"Can't you trade Selene back?"

"Daniel!" Mrs. O'Neill turned to me, obviously shocked. "You can't mean that."

"It's what Selene wants," I told her, surprised at her disapproval of my idea. "She said so herself. She wants to be with Auntie."

Before Mrs. O'Neill could say a word, Miss

Perkins said, "Didn't I just tell you—that girl is worn-out, used up. She's no good to Auntie—which is why she took your sister."

"Just take me to her," Selene begged. "Give me a chance to show her I can still do the chores."

Miss Perkins shook her head. "I know it ain't easy, but you got to make the best of your life here."

The old woman sat back in the rocker, her face now hidden in shadows. She was quiet for so long that I thought she'd fallen asleep. I looked at Mrs. O'Neill and whispered, "Should we leave?"

Miss Perkins must have heard me. "I ain't sleeping. I'm pondering." With surprising energy, she pushed herself up and out of the rocking chair. "You all come back here tomorrow afternoon. By then I might have an idea or two."

She walked to the door with us and watched Mrs. O'Neill help Selene with zippers and mittens. "The poor child," Miss Perkins said softly. "She's under a spell, like that girl who come back fifty year ago and died in the orphanage. When Auntie lets them go, they ain't long for this world."

Mrs. O'Neill stared at the old woman. "Please don't talk like that in front of the child."

Selene didn't seem to have heard. She was standing with her back to us, watching the cats racing each other up and down the steps.

Miss Perkins sighed. "Ain't none of that girl's fault my auntie took her. Must be something I can do to stop that old woman, her and that hog of hers."

She opened the door and ushered us out. "I'll see you tomorrow."

With that, we were on the porch with the door shut behind us. It was dark now, and the sliver of moon high above us didn't do much to light our way down the icy sidewalk to the car.

"Well," Mrs. O'Neill said as she started the engine. "I don't know what to make of the old woman."

"Do you trust her?" I asked.

Mrs. O'Neill bit her lower lip and eased the car over the ruts in the icy road. In the headlights I saw a skinny dog running along the sidewalk. He had something in his mouth—a scrap he'd found in the garbage, I guessed.

"I'm truly hoping she can get your sister back. How, I don't know—just so it doesn't involve trading one child for another."

She paused as she turned right from Railroad

Avenue onto Main Street. It was only five o'clock, but not a single store was open. Except for the streetlights and a traffic light set on blinking red, the town was dark.

"I'm also hoping we can keep Selene with us for a long time," she said.

I looked over my shoulder at the back seat. Selene was staring out the window, watching the buildings and houses slip past. Her face was pale and sad. The doll lay beside her as if she didn't care about it anymore. I think she knew then that she'd never see Auntie again.

SIXTEEN

As Mrs. O'Neill pulled her car into my driveway, she asked me if I'd like to have dinner at her house. "My daughter Eleanor will be here," she said. "It should be interesting to see what happens between her and Selene."

While Mrs. O'Neill and Selene waited, I ran into the house to ask permission. Dad was sitting on the couch by himself, staring into the fire. The room was dark.

Barely acknowledging me, he nodded. "Sure, sure, go ahead. I don't think your mother plans on cooking anything tonight."

"Where is she?"

He shrugged. "Upstairs, taking a nap."

"At five thirty?"

"Go on, Daniel. Don't keep Mrs. O'Neill waiting." He poured himself a glass of wine and went back to staring into the fire.

On the way out, I glanced upstairs, wondering if I should check on Mom. I decided against it and ran from the house to the warm car. Was this how it was going to be from now on? Mom upstairs sleeping, Dad drinking wine in the dark? I had to get my sister back.

"Is everything okay?" Mrs. O'Neill asked.

"Fine." I kept my head turned so she wouldn't see my face. One sympathetic look and I'd break down and tell her everything.

At the O'Neills' house, lights shone from windows and woodsmoke rose from the chimney into the cold night. Mrs. O'Neill helped Selene out of the car and led us inside. From the sounds and smells, I figured that Mr. O'Neill was busy in the kitchen. A tall gray-haired woman waited in the hallway as we took off our coats and jackets, scarves and hats and mittens. While she hugged her mother, Eleanor stared at Selene. She was so pale, I thought she might faint dead away.

Selene didn't so much as glance at Eleanor. Turning her back on all of us, she went into the living room, sat down near the fire, and began whispering to Little Erica.

"My God, Mother," Eleanor whispered. "She's fifty-seven years old, but she looks like she did on the day she disappeared. How can that be?"

"I warned you," Mrs. O'Neill said.

Eleanor took her mother's arm. I could almost smell her fear and confusion. "Do you think she'll remember me?"

"Maybe you should go sit beside her and tell her who you are."

Eleanor looked so scared, you'd have thought Selene was a ghost—which in a way I guessed she was, a girl come back from the dead unchanged.

"What's the matter?" Mrs. O'Neill asked.

Eleanor bit her lip just the way her mother did when she was nervous. "It's a shock, Mom, seeing her again, looking exactly the same. I recognize her, but how can she possibly recognize me?" She glanced uneasily at the child in the living room. "I don't know what to say, what to do."

"Selene needs our help, Eleanor. She's so unhappy, I fear she'll fade away from us altogether if we don't reach her." Mrs. O'Neill patted her daughter's arm. "Why don't you talk to her awhile — win her trust, maybe."

I watched Eleanor cross the room slowly. Sitting on the floor beside Selene, she smiled at her. "I'm Mrs. O'Neill's daughter Eleanor," she told her. "What's your name?"

Without looking at Eleanor, Selene said, "I'm called Girl."

Eleanor sent her mother an anxious glance. "I had a friend when I was your age," she told Selene. "She looked just like you."

"It wasn't me, if that's what you're thinking."

"Her name was Selene, and she lived right up the road. We played together every day."

"Well, I ain't never played with nobody. I worked every day and half the night for Auntie."

Eleanor glanced at her mother again. Mrs. O'Neill joined the two of them in front of the fire.

"Try to remember, Selene," she said gently. "You spent the first seven years of your life playing with Eleanor—hopscotch and jump rope and—"

Selene jumped to her feet, her face flushed with anger. "I declare I'm sick to death of hearing about that girl! My name ain't Selene. How many times I got to tell you?"

Mrs. O'Neill reached out to pat Selene's shoulder, but the girl pulled away from her. "Leave me be!"

Jumping to her feet, Selene ran from the room and up the stairs. Overhead, a door slammed shut.

Mrs. O'Neill started to go after her, but Eleanor stopped her. "You heard her, Mom. She wants us to leave her alone."

Mrs. O'Neill looked upstairs. Even with the door shut, we could hear Selene crying. "She's so unhappy, so confused. She needs someone to help her remember who she is."

"I don't know who she is, but she's *not* Selene," Eleanor said. "She can't be—it's simply not possible."

I could tell that Eleanor's attitude disappointed her mother. "You grew up here," Mrs. O'Neill said. "You know about Old Auntie. She's turned Selene loose and taken Daniel's sister."

"I'm sorry, but I don't believe those old stories anymore. Maybe that girl was abandoned in the woods and raised by wild animals. That's no more far-fetched than your explanation. Call Social Services. They'll know what to do."

Mrs. O'Neill stared at her daughter as if she didn't know her. "And let the child die like the one before her?"

Eleanor gathered up her coat and her purse. "I'm going home. Call me when you come to your senses."

Mr. O'Neill came in from the kitchen, wearing his chef's apron. "What's going on?" he said. "Surely you're not leaving before we eat. I roasted a chicken and made your favorite dressing."

But Eleanor went on zipping her parka. Her face was determined. "I'm sorry, Dad, but I can't stay in the same house with that girl. It's too upsetting."

"We were hoping you could help her," he said.

"There's nothing I can do for her." Eleanor took her mother's hands in hers. "Please hand her over to the authorities."

Mrs. O'Neill shook her head. "I can't do that. I *won't* do that. Selene stays here."

Eleanor released her mother's hands. "All right,

do what you think is best, but don't ask me to be involved." She went to the kitchen door, but before she opened it, she looked at her parents. "I'm sorry, I really am, but there's something very wrong with that child, and it scares me."

As Eleanor stepped out into the cold, dark night, Mrs. O'Neill followed her to the door, as if she meant to call her back.

Mr. O'Neill stopped her. "Give her time," he said. "Let her think about this. For fifty years she's believed that Selene was dead. And now—put yourself in Eleanor's place."

Mrs. O'Neill sighed. "Well, dinner is ready for those who want to eat."

Mr. O'Neill went to the foot of the stairs and called Selene. Silence. He called again. And again. After three tries, he climbed the steps and knocked on a door.

"Selene, dinner's ready. Come down and join us."

"I ain't hungry," she answered.

"It's roast chicken and mashed potatoes and green beans."

"I said I ain't hungry."

"We'll save some for you," he said.

While we ate, I glanced at the empty places set for Eleanor and Selene. I wished Eleanor had stayed and tried harder, but maybe Mr. O'Neill was right and she'd change her mind. I wished that Selene was sitting at her place, eating her food, and behaving like a normal girl.

But most of all, I wished that Erica was sitting beside me.

After dinner, Mr. O'Neill offered to drive me home. When we were alone in the car, he asked me how my folks were doing.

"Okay, I guess."

He looked at me. "Okay, you guess? That doesn't sound good."

We were heading down the driveway toward our house, which stood out stark and gray against the snowy fields. One light shone in Mom and Dad's bedroom window. The clock on the dashboard said eight fifteen. Too early for them to be in bed.

Mr. O'Neill parked beside the back porch. To my surprise, he walked up the steps with me. The door wasn't locked—in case Erica came home, Mom said.

"Dad? Mom?" I called. "It's me."

Nobody answered. The kitchen was dark and cold.

Mr. O'Neill went to the foot of the back stairs and called, "Ted, you up there?"

A door opened, and light from Dad's study spilled down the steps. "John, is that you?"

"Yep, I brought your boy home."

Dad appeared at the top of the steps, backlit so we couldn't see his face. "Good of you," he said to Mr. O'Neill. "Thanks. I hope he wasn't a nuisance."

"Oh, no, not at all. Daniel's no trouble."

I turned on the kitchen light and watched Dad come downstairs. "Where's Mom?" I asked.

"In bed, reading." He went to the cupboard and pulled out a whiskey bottle. "Have a drink, John."

Mr. O'Neill sat at the table, and Dad filled a couple of glasses. I opened a can of soda and started to join them, but Dad told me to go up to bed. I started to protest, but changed my mind and did what he said. Maybe a talk with Mr. O'Neill would be good for him.

Before I went to my room, I knocked on Mom's

door. "It's me, Daniel," I called softly. "Are you awake?"

"Come in," she said.

"Are you all right?" I asked. She didn't look all right—hair still uncombed, bags under her eyes, dressed in an old bathrobe over her pajamas. Huddled under blankets and quilts, she had the look of an invalid.

"Of course I am. Why do you ask?"

I shrugged, embarrassed. "You don't usually go to bed this early."

"The house is so cold. I can't get warm anywhere but here." She looked around the room. "Why did we move here? Why did I let your father talk me into it?" She pulled the covers up around her shoulders and stared at the black night pressing against the windows.

"Mom," I said. "I—"

"Who's downstairs with your father?" she interrupted.

"Mr. O'Neill. He brought me home."

"Did you see that girl at their house?"

"Yes. She's staying with them."

"She belongs in an institution." Mom handed me an empty wineglass. "Make yourself useful, Daniel. Go fill this up for me. Red, not white. I hate white wine in the winter."

I backed away from her, but she was staring out the window again. "Do you think she's out there somewhere? Will she come back? Will we see her again?" She began to cry. "I can't stand this. I can't bear it. I want my daughter. I want Erica!"

"Mom—"

"Go to bed, Daniel. Let me alone, please, just go away."

"But what about—" I held up the wineglass.

"No. I changed my mind. I don't want it." She lay down and hid her face in her pillows.

"Well, good night," I said.

When she didn't answer, I left the room and closed the door. What was I supposed to do? Nothing was right in our house. Not even me.

SEVENTEEN

The next day, Mrs. O'Neill picked me up around three. Selene huddled in the back seat, hugging the doll, her face mournful. Snowflakes drifted in the gray air, floating up and down, swirling like tiny moths.

By the time we parked in front of Miss Perkins's house, an inch of fluffy snow coated the old snow, making it look fresh and new. We walked to the front door silently. No one had said much during the ride into Woodville. I think we were each locked in our own thoughts, wondering what Miss Perkins might tell us. Each of us hoping, hoping, hoping . . .

We waited on the cold porch for at least five minutes before the door opened and Miss Perkins stepped aside to let us enter. Three cats shot out of the house and two ran in.

Inside, it was as dark and cold and smelly as before. A small fire burned low on the hearth, but we didn't take off our coats.

For a while, no one spoke. It was as if we were waiting for Miss Perkins to tell us something and she was waiting for us to tell her something. A black cat crept into her lap, and two more emerged from the shadows to crouch at her feet. They watched us steadily, unblinking. I wondered how she told them apart.

The fire popped and crackled, and the wind did its best to squeeze in through every crack. Selene coughed. Mrs. O'Neill crossed and uncrossed her ankles. Somewhere in the back of the house, a cat yowled. *There must be dozens of them,* I thought, mostly black, gray, and dark tabbies.

"This is how it is," Miss Perkins said suddenly. "Selene, there's no way you can go back to my auntie. She don't want you no more. You must learn to live in the here and now—or die. Them's your choices. If I was you, I'd choose to live."

Tears ran down Selene's face, but she said nothing. She simply sat and stared as if she were a cat too, half wild, not one you dared to pet.

Miss Perkins turned her eyes to me. "She means to keep your sister for fifty years," she said, "just like she kept Selene and all the ones before her."

"There must be something you can do," I whispered. "My family is wrecked. My mother, my father—" I couldn't go on without losing my self-control and throwing myself at her feet, crying and begging for her help.

"I didn't say there's no way to get your sister back." Miss Perkins spoke so sharply, the cat on her lap raised its head, startled out of its nap.

"Have you actually spoken to her?" Mrs. O'Neill asked.

"Not exactly." Miss Perkins stroked the cat on her lap. "I got my ways of finding out things on the sly. Things folks don't want me to know. Things I don't want them to know I'm interested in."

Mrs. O'Neill nodded as if she understood, but

like me, I was sure she didn't quite see what the old woman meant. But she was a witch, and we weren't, so why should we expect to understand?

Miss Perkins stretched a hand toward Selene. "Bring me that dolly, dear."

Selene gripped the doll. "What do you want with her? She's mine."

The old woman leaned toward Selene and stared into her eyes. "The dolly," she said. "Give me the dolly."

The air seemed charged with electricity, and my skin tingled as if a thunderstorm were rolling through the house. I wanted to jump up and run from the dark room and the craziness of the old woman, but something kept me where I was.

Selene rose slowly and gave the doll to Miss Perkins. "Good girl," she said as Selene backed away and collapsed on the sofa. Mrs. O'Neill put her arm around her. For once, Selene did not pull away.

In the meantime, Miss Perkins turned the doll this way and that, studying her intently in the dim light of the fire. She caressed Little Erica, moved her arms and legs, and hummed to herself, as if she'd forgotten we were in the room. After a minute or so, she bent her head over the cat in her lap and seemed to listen. He made a strange sound, not a meow, not a growl, not a purr, but something like all three. She nodded her head slowly.

At last Miss Perkins looked up. Her eyes seemed unfocused, as if she weren't seeing us or the room, but was looking at something far away. Selene and I moved closer to Mrs. O'Neill. She held us both tightly.

Miss Perkins slowly came back to the room and the fire and the three of us. Her sharp eyes fixed themselves on me. "Come here, boy. Come close."

Even though I wanted to stay where I was, safe and warm beside Mrs. O'Neill, I did as she said. The old woman smelled of dried grass and herbs and flowers. A nice smell. I sniffed and breathed it in, feeling it spread through me like magic.

"How much do you want your sister back, boy?" she whispered. Her eyes probed mine.

"I'd do anything to get her away from Auntie."

"Will you go to Auntie's cabin tonight, all by yourself? No mammy, no pappy, nobody. All by yourself. Just you. Are you brave enough?"

I stared at her, almost speechless. "Tonight?"

"You said you want your sister back. You said you'll do anything. This is the onliest way to do it."

I glanced at Mrs. O'Neill to see what she thought. Her eyes were open but unfocused, as blank as Little Erica's eyes. She and Selene seemed to be in a trance.

Miss Perkins leaned toward me and studied my face. "You brave enough? 'Cause if you ain't, you'll never see your sister till fifty years from now. And that one there will be soon be dead." She nodded at Selene. "It's for both these girls you're doing it. You break the spell for your sister, you break it for Selene, too. Once the spell's broke, Auntie will be finished. The dark will take her."

I tried to stand tall and straight. Maybe if I acted brave, I'd be brave. "What do I have to do?" My voice came out in a squeak.

"You go to the door of the cabin at midnight — not one minute earlier, not one minute later. Knock three times. Auntie will call out, 'Who's that knock, knock, knocking at my door?' You'll say, 'A poor traveler lost in the cold.' She'll say, 'What you want with me?' You'll say, 'To sit by your fire a spell.'"

Miss Perkins stroked the cat's black fur and

crooned to him. Except for the wind and the fire, the room was as still as death.

"She'll ask you to tell her a riddle," she went on. "First you say, 'I brung you a cherry without a stone.'" Miss Perkins reached into her pocket and drew out a blossom. She laid it carefully on the table beside her. "A cherry don't have a stone when it's blooming."

"Second, say, 'I brung you a chicken without a bone.'" Miss Perkins took an egg from her pocket and laid it beside the blossom. "A chicken don't have bones while it's in the egg."

"They're old riddles," she said. "Everyone knows the answers, so she'll ask for something harder, a riddle she's never heard before."

The old woman coughed and sniffed and fidgeted with the doll. "Last of all, say, 'I brung you a servant that never tires and never grows old.'" She added Little Erica to the objects on the table.

"It ain't a riddle she'll have heard before. If she can't guess the answer in three tries, she's got to open the door and let you in."

My heart knocked about in my chest, hammering and pounding my ribs. "But when she sees me, she'll know who I am."

"Auntie ain't the onliest one that knows her way around the dark side of the moon. I got tricks of my own, boy. She won't know you. I'll see to that."

The cat interrupted her with an odd, questioning sort of noise. Miss Perkins stroked him till he purred loud enough to make my bones vibrate.

"Soon as you're through the door," she went on, "Auntie will ask you for the answer to the riddle. Open the sack and show her the servant that never tires and never grows old. Once she sees that dolly, she'll forget about your sister. At least for a while—"

"But—" I couldn't stop myself from interrupting the old woman again. "She *knows* the doll belongs to Erica. And how can a doll be a servant? She's plastic, she's not alive, she can't move or talk or—"

"Hush up and quit asking fool questions. You got to trust me, boy. Get your sister out of the cabin as fast as you can. She won't want to come. You'll have to drag her away. Run for home like you got wings on your heels or seven-league boots on your feet."

"But what if—"

"Don't vex me no more, boy. Do what I tell you, bring your sister home, and the spell will bust at sunrise—for both girls. They'll remember who they are in this world, but they won't remember nothing about Auntie's world." Miss Perkins scrunched her face into a tight fist, and the cat lashed his tail and hissed at me.

My brain whirled with questions, but my voice had dried up and my mouth felt numb, the way it does in the dentist's office when he gives you Novocain. I nodded, as if I understood, and hoped I'd be able to do all she asked.

Miss Perkins put my sister's doll into a burlap sack, tied it shut, and gave it to me. "No matter what, don't open this sack until you're inside the cabin, and don't be scairt of the dolly."

Before I could ask her why I'd be scared of a doll, she gave me a warning look, and I shut my mouth.

Miss Perkins nodded, took a deep breath, and let it out slowly. "Now go sit on that sofa and keep your mouth shut about everything I done told you."

I took my place next to Mrs. O'Neill, who continued to stare straight ahead at nothing I could see.

Miss Perkins murmured a few words to the cat. The moment he closed his eyes, Mrs. O'Neill and Selene came back from wherever they'd been. They stretched and yawned as if they'd been napping.

Selene looked bewildered, as if she wasn't quite sure where she was. Although I expected her to ask about the doll, she didn't say a word.

"Thank you for your time," Mrs. O'Neill said to Miss Perkins. "I'm sorry you can't do anything to help us. That poor child—fifty years is a long time."

"The years will go by in a flash." Miss Perkins picked up a ball of yarn and her knitting—a lumpy black scarf already long enough to wrap two or three times around her neck.

Gently helping Selene to her feet, Mrs. O'Neill turned to me. "Come along, Daniel. The snow's getting worse. Your parents must be worried."

"See yourselves out," Miss Perkins said. "I'm a mite weary tonight. When you're old as me, the cold settles in your bones and sets them to aching and scraping against each other."

"Good night, then," Mrs. O'Neill said. "Take care of yourself, Miss Perkins."

"You, too, dearie, and don't fret yourself about the snow. It'll stop soon enough."

We left Miss Perkins sitting by the fire, knitting and humming to herself while the cat dozed on her lap. Outside, the cold air froze the hairs in my nose, and my eyes watered, but I was glad to be away from the smoky smell of the house.

I kept the sack behind my back, but no one noticed it. Selene sat behind me with her nose pressed against the window and watched the empty streets of Woodville glide past. A flake or two of snow drifted past the windshield, but Miss Perkins was right—the moon was already breaking through the clouds.

As usual, our house looked dark and vacant. As it had the previous night, a lamp glimmered in Mom's bedroom window, but the downstairs windows were lit only by the headlights of the car.

Mrs. O'Neill stared at the house. "My goodness, Daniel, is anyone home?"

"They're upstairs," I said. "The light's on in the bedroom. Dad's office is in the back—that's where he is." Where he always is—lost in computer games and websites for missing children.

As I opened the car door, she asked, "Do you want me to come in with you?"

"No, it's okay. Everything's fine." What a good liar I was getting to be. "Thanks for taking me to see Miss Perkins again."

While we talked, I was aware of Selene watching

me through the window. I waved to her, but she turned away.

Mrs. O'Neill said goodbye and turned around slowly, her headlights washing over the unpainted sides of our house. I watched the taillights grow small as the car disappeared around the curve in the driveway.

The kitchen looked the way it always did. Sink full of dirty dishes. Trash can overflowing with pizza boxes, beer cans, and wine bottles. Table littered with newspapers, paper plates, coffee cups, forks and knives and spoons, an empty wine bottle, ashtrays heaped with cigarette butts.

"Dad? Mom?" I called.

"Up here," Dad answered.

I climbed the back stairs slowly, keeping the sack behind my back. It was the new normal—Dad playing a war game on the computer, Mom huddled in her room under a quilt, reading.

"We saved some pizza for you," Mom said. "It's in the fridge. Just heat it up in the microwave."

"Thanks." I stowed the sack under my bed and went down to the kitchen to warm up the pizza. The crust tasted like burned cardboard and the cheese had turned to something that resembled melted plastic and stuck to my teeth, but I ate it anyway. I was going to be out in the cold a long time. I needed something in my belly.

For a while I sat at the table and watched the clock. Seven p.m., eight p.m.—time crept past. Upstairs, my parents were silently engrossed in their books and games.

I said good night to them and went to my room. They barely acknowledged my presence. It was as if I'd disappeared too. If I failed tonight, if Bloody Bones killed and ate me, would they care? Would they send anyone to look for me? Or would they just sink deeper and deeper into the house, burrowing under blankets, eating bad pizza, drinking, smoking, not even noticing I was gone?

For at least an hour I stood at my window, trying to remember the way our family used to be, but only seeing myself teasing Erica and making her cry, forcing her to leave the doll in the woods. Why had I been so mean to her?

I shivered in the cold air that leaked through the

loose windowpanes and watched the wind blow the clouds away. The moon sailed into sight and shone on the snowy fields. In its bright light I saw the beginning of the path that led to Auntie's cabin.

I glanced at my clock. Ten thirty. It was time to go.

EIGHTEEN

I hauled the burlap sack out from under the bed, grabbed a flashlight, and tiptoed downstairs. Even though I'd heard Dad go to bed and I knew Mom was with him, the house felt empty, so dark and cold and silent I could hear my own breathing. I pulled one of Erica's old jackets off the coatrack, grabbed a pair of mittens, a hat, and her red boots, and stuffed everything into a backpack. Zipping my parka, I stepped into the darkness. The cold wind hit me like a fist, and the freezing air hurt my chest.

Crouched in the snow, I took a long look at the house. Then with my head down, I ran across the field and into the woods. No one but deer and small animals had walked on the path since it snowed, so I slipped and slid and sank to my knees over and over again, clambering out of one snowdrift and stumbling into another.

The burlap sack made everything worse. With every step I took, it grew heavier. I didn't understand how the doll could weigh so much. Maybe plowing through the snow was taking all my energy, leaving me tired and weak legged.

I was about to open the sack to make sure something else wasn't in there—a few boulders maybe—but I remembered what Miss Perkins had told me. If I wanted to rescue Erica, I had to do exactly what the old woman said.

By the time I reached the trail to the top of Brewster's Hill, I was exhausted. There was no protection from the wind. Snow blew in my face. Hard, icy pellets stung my skin and made my forehead ache. Every now and then I glimpsed shadowy shapes in the darkness—deer, I hoped.

There were noises, too—owls, foxes, and the low mutters of other things, growling and snarling, squealing and yelping in the woods. Brody told me there were wild hogs up here, razorbacks like Bloody Bones. I told myself it wasn't the monster hog I heard out there, but my knees shook with fear.

The sack grew so heavy I could barely drag it uphill. Gasping for breath, I thought it was like a backpack that never weighed much when I left home, but grew heavier after an hour or so of hiking. I felt like Atlas carrying the world on my shoulders.

Again I was tempted to open the sack and take out whatever was weighing it down, but when I started fumbling with the rope that held it closed, I swear I heard Miss Perkins's voice in the wind telling me not to do it. I sighed and began climbing again, dragging the sack behind me.

When I finally reached the top of the hill, it was almost midnight. Stunned, I stared at the scene before me. No longer in ruins, the cabin looked like something in a fairy tale. Snow covered its roof, icicles hung from its eves, smoke rose from its chimney, and candles glowed in its windows.

I crept closer, scared that Old Auntie would hear my footsteps. After hiding my backpack behind a rock near the cabin, I laid the sack down by the cabin door, glad to be relieved of its weight. Shadows cast by the windblown trees made the sack seem to be moving. Uneasily, I edged away from it. It wasn't a trick of the shadows. The sack had begun to move, as if something inside wanted to get out.

I heard Old Auntie walking around inside the cabin, berating someone in a harsh voice. "Lazy girl, stupid girl," she said. "You ain't worth a wooden nickel. The girl afore you done all I asked and more, but you act like you never scrubbed a pot in your life."

I heard a smack and a low cry. "Don't hit me, Auntie. I'm doing my best." *Erica,* I thought, *Erica's in there.* Yet I stood at the door like a statue, afraid to raise my hand and knock.

"Well, your best ain't good enough, is it?" Another slap. Another cry from my sister.

The moon cast my shadow on the door, making me seem much larger than I was. I forced myself to knock three times.

From inside, a shrill voice called, "Who's that knock, knock, knocking at my door?"

"A poor traveler lost in the cold." Fear made it hard to keep my voice steady.

"What do you want with me?"

"To sit by your fire a spell."

"Ask me a riddle, and maybe I'll let you in."

I took a deep breath. Hoping I remembered the words, I said, "I brung you a cherry without a stone."

"A cherry when it's blooming, it has no stone," Old Auntie answered. "Ask me another that ain't so easy."

"I brung you a chicken that has no bone."

"Hah, another easy one—a chicken when it's pipping, it has no bone." Old Auntie laughed. "Now you tell me one I ain't heard, laddie, and make it snappy."

"I brung you a servant that never tires and never grows old." At my feet, the sack lurched wildly, and a harsh voice cried, "Let me out!"

I backed away in horror, but inside the cabin, all was silence. Auntie must have been mulling over the riddle. "A servant that never tires and never grows old?"

"Yes, ma'am."

The sack heaved. "Let me out!"

"Is the answer *time*?" Auntie called.

"No, ma'am."

Another silence. "You sure it's not *time*?"

"Yes, ma'am."

"That's right. Time ain't nobody's servant," she muttered. "T'other way round, I reckon." Another moment of silence. "How about water? Is that the answer?"

"No, ma'am."

Again the sack twitched with life. Again the voice cried, "Let me out!"

"Is it fire, then?" Auntie asked through the door.

"No, none of them is right, ma'am." That was three wrong guesses. She had to let me in.

Sure enough, a key jiggled in a lock and the door slowly opened. The old woman who'd terrified me in the woods poked her head out.

Spotting the sack, she asked, "What's in that there gunnysack?"

"The answer to the riddle," I told her. "Let me in and you'll see."

She stepped back, and I dragged the sack inside.

It was all I could do to manage it. It humped up and swayed from side to side. Something in that sack was definitely alive.

Behind Old Auntie, my sister crouched by the fire. Although I'd told myself that Erica might not look like herself, I had no idea she'd be almost un-recognizable. Thin and pale, dirty and barefoot, her hair an uncombed thicket of tangles, she wore a col-orless, shapeless dress that hung loosely from her bony frame. More than anyone else, she looked like Selene—the same sullen expression on her face, the same fear, the same exhaustion. She could have been Selene's twin.

It was clear that she didn't know me, and judging by the look in her eyes, she didn't trust me either. How was I to get her out of the cabin and drag her all the way home?

Auntie must have noticed me staring at Erica, because she said, "Don't pay her no mind. She ain't nobody. Just Girl. The worst servant I ever had. Don't know the meaning of work."

Hiding her face, Erica fed twigs into the fire. "I'm sorry, Auntie," she whispered. "I do my best."

"I told you your best ain't nearly good enough, Girl." Old Auntie started struggling with the rope that tied the sack closed. "There's something alive in here," she cried. "It wants out. Get away, laddie. Let's see what you brung me."

She shoved me aside. At the moment I was more scared of the doll than I was of Old Auntie.

"It's my servant, ain't it? The answer to that there riddle about never getting tired and never getting old."

She tore the sack open, and the doll jumped out. It was the size of Erica herself, but it looked nothing like Little Erica. Its hair was tangled and fell over its bony face like a thicket of brambles. Its arms were long and skinny, its sharp nails like claws. It wore tatters of clothing, stained and faded. The fabric was so thin I saw its ribs.

With a grin as wicked as death, the conjure woman laughed with delight and picked up the doll. "Why, ain't you the ugliest little critter I ever did see!"

"Let me down, Auntie, let me down!" As soon as its feet hit the floor, it grabbed a broom and began sweeping, running this way and that like a wind-up toy, lurching and bumping into things, knocking furniture over, breaking bowls, scattering Auntie's things like leaves in a winter storm.

"Auntie, Auntie," it cried, "catch me if you can!"

While Auntie chased it around the cabin, I grabbed Erica and hauled her toward the door. Just as I expected, she fought the way Selene had, kicking, scratching, biting. It was like holding a wild animal.

"Auntie!" she screamed. "Auntie!"

But the old woman was too busy to notice what was happening. Or maybe she didn't care about my sister now that she had a new servant. She caught the creature and slapped its face hard.

"Bad girl," she screamed, and shook it until its bones rattled and its head bobbed. "Look what you done!"

Once Erica and I were outside, I held her still, forced her arms into the jacket's sleeves, and zipped up the front. I jammed the hat on her head, but she kicked so hard I couldn't get the boots on her feet. Abandoning them, I snatched up my backpack and dragged my sister toward the trail.

"Auntie, Auntie!" she shrieked.

"What's wrong with you?" I shook her. "We've got to get away from here."

"Leave me be. I don't want to go anywhere!"

"I'm your brother. I've come to take you home."

"Liar! You ain't my brother. I don't have no brother. I got no one save for Auntie—no home but here!" Erica thrashed and flailed and kicked. "Let me go! Let me go!"

I held her tight and kept going, stumbling through the snow. Behind us, I heard a sort of grunting, squealing, growling sound. I looked back and saw Bloody Bones come out of the trees. The moon shone on his bald head and cast his shadow across the snow. His ragged clothes fluttered in the wind. I saw his bones and his claws and his sharp teeth.

Even though Erica slowed me down, I ran and jumped over the snow, going as fast as I could. Bloody Bones wasn't going to stop me from bringing my sister home and making things right again.

Behind us, the cabin door opened, and Old Auntie screamed, "Get them, dear boy, bring them back to me!"

"No, Auntie," Erica cried. "Don't sic him on me! I'll work hard, I'll do things right, I promise!"

Still struggling to keep hold of my sister, I slipped and slid down the trail, trying to keep us from falling. The wind blew us toward the edge of the drop-off, roots and stones rose up to trip us, but I kept going, forcing Erica to keep up with me.

Bloody Bones crashed through the snow behind us, gaining on us with every step. I imagined his breath as foul as death itself, his sharp claws squeezing around my throat, his eyeless skull looming over me in the moonlight.

"Don't let them get away!" Old Auntie's voice mingled with the wind shrieking through the trees. "Stop them—they'll bring us both to ruin."

Bloody Bones snuffled and snorted. His bones rattled. He was gaining on us. I felt him grab at my jacket and miss. I tried to run faster, but a stone turned under my foot, and I fell. I lost my grip on Erica and lay stunned.

Above me stood Bloody Bones. While I lay in the snow staring up at him, he threw back his head and snorted. Then he bent down and pulled me to my feet. His bear claws sank into my shoulders. His face was so close I could see his tusks and his panther fangs and his empty eye sockets. The stink of him made me gag.

His bones rattled as he lifted me above his head. He was going to throw me off the cliff.

Just as he tensed to hurl me into the valley, I heard the crack of something hard hit Bloody Bones. He staggered backward, away from the edge of the cliff, and lost his hold on me. One leg collapsed, and he fell with a clatter of bones.

As he struggled to stand, another rock hit him. This one broke his arm clean off. The shattered bones dropped into the snow. Howling with anger, Bloody Bones lunged toward me, his one arm outstretched to push me to my death, his right leg useless.

Without thinking of anything but surviving, I dodged away from him. Unable to stop in time, Bloody Bones plunged over the edge of the cliff, screaming as he bounced from rock to rock, his bones flying apart and scattering as he went. In seconds, he was gone, leaving only the echo of his scream.

Auntie hobbled down the trail toward us. "My

boy, my dear boy!" she screamed, her face and voice filled with rage and sorrow. "What have you done, you miserable, wicked creature?"

I backed away, but it wasn't me the conjure woman was speaking to. Erica stood behind me. Pale and trembling, she held a rock in each hand.

Old Auntie flung a string of strange words at both of us, but the wind turned them back on her. Raising her hands as if to fend off what she'd said, she began backing slowly up the trail.

"What will I do now without my dear boy?" she cried.

With each step she took, the wind blew harder and her shadow grew fainter, her body less solid. By the time she vanished into the woods, she was almost transparent.

"Auntie." Erica stretched her arms toward the old woman. "Auntie. I'm sorry. Don't leave me. I only meant to stop him from hurting the boy."

Seizing my sister's arm, I yanked her down the trail. She was still struggling when she looked back and screamed, "The cabin's on fire. It's burning! Put it out! Save her!"

I spun around. At the top of Brewster's Hill, flames leaped into the air, lighting the bare trees with an orange glow, sending sparks shooting toward the winter sky.

With a burst of strength, Erica broke away from me and ran up the trail. I ran after her, but this time she was too fast for me. I caught up with her at the cabin.

Or what was left of it. The old rotten wood had exploded in flames and burned so fast that the fire was already flickering over charred logs. Smoke blew sideways in the wind. Embers scattered. I kept a firm grip on Erica to keep her from running into the ruins to rescue Auntie.

"She's gone," I said. Dead and gone, I hoped. Burned to ashes. "You can't do anything for her now."

Erica collapsed against me, sobbing. "Now I got nobody. No home. Nothing."

The fight had gone out of her. I held her tight and wondered if I'd ever hugged her before. I couldn't remember, but I kind of doubted it. Right now, though, I wanted to hold her for a long time, never let her go, never let anything bad ever happen to her again.

"You have me," I told her, "and Mom and Dad."

She shook her head and snuffled. "I ain't got nobody," she insisted. "No brother, no sister, no mother, no father."

In tears, she pulled away from me and stumbled down the trail. She had nothing more to say, and neither did I.

As we came out of the woods, I pointed to our house, a dark box in the field, moonlight glinting off the glass in its windows

"That's where we live," I told her. "You and me and Mom and Dad."

"I never saw that house. I never lived there." Her voice was as dull and lifeless as Selene's, but she let me lead her into the kitchen.

"Mom, Dad!" I shouted. "Come down here."

Upstairs, a bed creaked, footsteps crossed the floor, a door opened. "Daniel," Dad called, "what are you shouting about? It's three a.m."

"Come see!" In a few seconds I'd be a hero, the boy who rescued his sister from the old conjure woman. They'd be so happy, so proud of me. I could hardly wait for them to see Erica.

Dad fumbled with the hall light and came slowly

downstairs, barely awake, from the sound of it. He stopped halfway and stared at Erica. "What's that girl doing here? I thought she was staying with the O'Neills. Your mother won't—"

I stared at him, shocked. "Dad, it's Erica. I found her!"

"Are you crazy?" Dad asked. "Have you completely lost your mind?"

Mom appeared behind him. "Why did you bring that creature here? I won't have her in this house!"

Erica scowled at me. "Didn't I tell you? I'm not your sister. They don't want me. They don't love me. It's just like Auntie said."

She pulled away from me and ran toward the back door, but I grabbed her before she opened it. Holding her tight, I made her face Mom and Dad.

"Please look at her," I told them. "She's been living with a crazy old woman up on Brewster's Hill, and she doesn't remember anything about us—just like Selene. But she's Erica."

"She can't be," Mom whispered. Dad shook his head. With his back to Erica and me, he stared out the kitchen window at the black night.

How could they not recognize their own daughter? Yes, she was dirty, her hair uncombed. She was thin and pale, obviously in the same state as Selene, but under it all, she was my sister and their daughter, the one they'd been mourning for almost a week.

Erica began to cry. "Let me go," she begged. "I don't belong here, I don't belong anywhere, I might as well be dead."

"Please don't talk like that." Slowly Mom reached out and touched Erica's shoulder. "I don't know who you are, but I can't bear to see a child so unhappy."

Erica collapsed against Mom's side. Her bare feet were blue with cold. Her face was bruised, and she was shaking hard enough to make her teeth chatter. "I'm so tired," she whispered. "Please can I sleep by your fire till morning? I promise I won't be no bother. If you got work for me to do, I'll do it. I'll sweep. I'll scrub floors. I'll chop wood."

"You'll do no such thing," Mom said. "You're in no condition to work for us or anyone else."

"And you certainly won't sleep by the fire," Dad said.

"Auntie says my place is on the hearth," Erica said, "by the fire. It's warm there, and I don't mind the hard floor no more."

"You poor child. I don't know who your aunt is, but she's not fit to take care of you." Dad bent down and picked Erica up. She lay as limp as a kitten in his arms, her eyes half closed. "She hardly weighs anything," he said.

I watched him carry her upstairs to her room. She was asleep before Mom covered her with her lavender checked comforter. Mom and Dad stood together, looking down at her, their eyes full of questions.

NINETEEN

At dawn, Erica's cries woke me with a jolt that nearly knocked me out of bed. "Mommy!" she screamed. "Mommy!"

I ran into the hall and followed Mom and Dad into Erica's bedroom. My sister flung herself at Mom, crying hysterically. Over her head, Mom stared at Dad, her eyes wide with shock. Both looked as if they were sleepwalking—groggy, unsteady, trembling.

"Erica, oh, Erica," Mom cried. "It's you. It really *is* you. Oh, darling, you've come home at last."

"We thought we'd lost you," Dad whispered.

"And then, when Daniel brought you home, we, we" — his voice broke for a second — "we didn't even recognize you."

I don't think Erica heard a word my parents said. She was still caught in the snares of her dream. "Hold me tight, Mommy. Don't let Auntie come for me. Keep her away."

Mom rocked Erica as if she were a baby, murmured to her, held her tight. "We won't let anyone take you away."

Gradually Erica stopped crying, but she shivered and shook and looked around fearfully, as if she expected to see Auntie's face at the window.

"You're safe now," Dad said. "Don't be afraid. It was just a dream."

It was then that Erica noticed her hands. "Why are my hands so dirty?" Pulling away from Mom, she stared at her reflection in the mirror over her bureau. A wild-eyed girl with tangled hair and a dirty, bruised face stared back at her. "What's happened to me?"

Mom looked at Dad as if she wasn't sure what to say.

"You've been missing for almost a week," Dad finally said.

"Daniel found you on Brewster's Hill last night," Mom added, "and brought you home."

"What were you doing up there in the cold?" Dad asked. "We've searched every square inch of the woods, the creeks, the lakes, and no one found a trace of you. And now you're here. It's a miracle."

Erica looked puzzled. "I was looking for my doll with Daniel. We couldn't find her—someone took her."

Pausing to catch her breath, Erica spread her fingers and studied her broken nails and the dirt ground into her skin. With a shudder, she flung herself back into Mom's arms. "And then someone took *me*."

Mom held Erica, hugging her and stroking her hair. "No, no," she murmured. "You were lost, but now you're home. We'll never let anyone take you from us."

We sat with Erica for a long time, soothing her, calming her. At last, just as morning light filled the room, she relaxed and fell asleep.

Mom told Dad and me to go to bed. "I'll stay

and watch over her," she whispered. "I don't want her to wake up frightened again."

Even though it was morning, I did what Mom said. I was warm and safe. I'd brought my sister home, and she was sleeping in her own bed. As soon as I pulled up the covers, I dropped into sleep like a stone falling into a well.

When I came downstairs, Dad was in the kitchen. While I'd been sleeping, he'd shaved, showered, and exchanged his sweatpants for jeans and his sweatshirt for a wool sweater. He'd washed the dishes and taken out the trash. He'd swept the floor and scrubbed the countertops. The smell of freshly made coffee filled the air.

"You must not have gone back to bed," I said.

"I couldn't sleep, so I cleaned up the place." He poured himself a cup of coffee and sat down at the table. "I apologize for not believing you, Daniel," he said, "but you have to admit your story sounded like something out of a fairy tale—old conjure women roaming the mountains, stealing children, keeping them for fifty years. I'm a practical man, a rational man. I've never believed in the supernatural."

He frowned and rubbed his chin. Except for the uncertainty in his eyes, he looked like himself. "I'd never have believed in Old Auntie when we lived in Connecticut, but here, well, crazy as it sounds, I can't come up with any other explanation."

I looked at him, surprised. "You *believe* me?"

"Like I said, what other explanation is there? Erica couldn't have survived on her own in this cold. There's no evidence that she was kidnapped by a passing stranger. Her dream fits in with what you've told me about that conjure woman or witch—or whatever she is or was."

He drank more coffee and stared past me at nothing in particular. "And then there's Selene," he added. "Surely the O'Neills are too sane to believe in old stories unless there's some truth to them."

Before I could say a word, someone began pounding on the back door. "Mama," a voice cried. "Daddy, it's me. Let me in, let me in!"

Dad was so startled, he almost spilled what was left of his coffee, but I jumped up and flung the door open. Selene stood on the porch, staring at me.

"Who are you?" she asked. "What are you doing

in my house? Where's my mother? Who's that man at the table?"

"Don't you remember me?"

"I've never seen you in my life." Pushing me aside, she headed toward the back stairs. "Mama, Daddy, it's me," she called. "Where are you?"

Before Selene was halfway up the steps, Mrs. O'Neill followed her into the kitchen. "Wait," she cried to the nearly hysterical girl. "I need to tell you something."

Selene ignored her. "Mama!" she screamed. "Mama!"

Her eyes darted around the kitchen. "What have you done with our table? Where are our chairs? And the clock on the wall and the calendar by the door and the curtains Mama made?"

Dodging Mrs. O'Neill, she ran into the hall. We heard her go from room to room, her feet clattering across the floor. "This isn't right. This isn't our couch, not our chairs—where's the wallpaper? Mama! Daddy!" Her voice rose with every word.

Mrs. O'Neill caught her at the foot of the front stairway. "Selene, Selene, I know everything seems wrong and you're scared, but you must be still and listen to me."

"What are you and those other people doing in my house?" Selene cried. "Why have you changed all the furniture? Where's my mother and my father and Nadine?"

"Please, please, Selene, let me explain."

Mrs. O'Neill managed to lead the girl into the living room. "Here," she said gently. "Sit with me, and I'll tell you the best I can."

Selene sat on the edge of the couch and stared at Mrs. O'Neill. Her face pale, her eyes huge, she asked, "Has something terrible happened to them? Is that it?"

"Oh, my dear child," Mrs. O'Neill said sadly. "I hardly know where to begin."

Silently I went back to the kitchen. Dad had made another pot of coffee. Upstairs, Mom was giving Erica a bath. In the living room, Mrs. O'Neill murmured to Selene. For now, at least, the house was quiet—the way it used it to be.

We sat together silently, Dad and I. Neither of us knew what to say. He drank his coffee and stared out the window, his face expressionless.

I'd had time to adjust to the reality of witchcraft and spells and hogs that walked on their hind legs, but just a few hours earlier Old Auntie had turned my parents' beliefs about the nature of reality upside down. Maybe they should visit Miss Perkins. She could explain the way things were in Woodville.

I heard footsteps on the stairs. Scrubbed clean, her hair washed, brushed, and combed, wearing clean clothes, Erica seemed to be exactly the same as before—until you saw the bruises on her face, until you looked into her eyes and saw the shadows there. She'd been somewhere only she and Selene knew about.

Mom had washed *her* hair, too, and finally changed her clothes. Like Erica, she seemed her old self, the mother I knew, except her face had wrinkles I hadn't noticed before and there were new gray streaks in her hair.

Erica sat beside me. "You look really nice," I told her.

She put her hands over her face to hide the bruises. "I look awful."

Mom opened a catalog and showed Erica a page.

"I know how much you loved your doll," she said. "We can order another one just like her."

With a look of horror, Erica shoved the catalog away so fast she knocked over the glass of orange juice Dad had set in front of her. "Get that picture away from me," she shouted. "I hate that doll. Throw the catalog away. Burn it up!"

"But Erica," Mom began.

"No!"

When Erica began to cry, Mom hugged her. "It's all right, honey. I just thought . . ." Her voice trailed away as she stroked Erica's hair.

I glanced at the catalog lying open on the floor. There she was, Little Erica, red hair and all. *Oh, Mom,* I thought, *if you only knew* . . . I picked up the catalog and carried it to the garbage can. No more Little Erica.

Once Erica calmed down, Dad asked, "Who wants pancakes for breakfast?" He seemed to be making a huge effort to act as if this were an ordinary morning.

Mrs. O'Neill appeared in the doorway. "Did we hear something about pancakes?"

Pale and quiet, Selene followed her into the kitchen. While Dad stirred the batter, Mrs. O'Neill urged Selene to join us at the table, but she shook her head and held back.

"Who's that?" Erica asked.

"Selene," Mom said. "She lives down the road with Mr. and Mrs. O'Neill."

"She's your age," I told Erica.

Erica slid out of her chair and crossed the room. Taking Selene's hand, she said, "Come sit beside me. We're going to be friends, you and me. I just know it."

Erica led Selene to the chair next to hers. "Do you like pancakes?"

Selene nodded. "With maple syrup."

"Coming right up." Dad set plates in front of Erica and Selene, and Mom passed them the syrup.

Before either girl picked up her fork, they studied each other for at least a minute. They didn't say a word, but I sensed something flowing back and forth between them. Slowly Erica put her hand on Selene's hand and smiled at her. Selene smiled back.

It was the first time I'd ever seen that girl look happy.

After breakfast, Erica took her new friend upstairs. I heard Selene say, "You sleep in my old room." Then the door closed behind them.

I looked around the quiet kitchen, which was neat and orderly again. Sunlight filled corners that once were dark. No whispers disturbed the silence.

Mrs. O'Neill took a sip of coffee. "I believe those girls will be good friends."

Mom smiled. "Erica needs a friend."

"So does Selene," Mrs. O'Neill said.

After a little silence Mrs. O'Neill added, "Thank goodness, they've both forgotten Auntie and all that happened to them in that cabin."

Except in dreams, I thought. *Except in dreams.*

TWENTY

A few days later, Brody showed up. It was the first time he'd been in our house, and he spent some time looking around and making comments like "Your roof's leaking, that's why that brown stain's on your ceiling" or "You better get your dad to put some putty in them window frames. You're letting cold air in and warm air out. That'll run your heat bill sky-high."

Of course, what he'd really come for was to see Erica, who was helping Mom clean the living room—

she'd been doing chores ever since she came back from Old Auntie's.

"She looks real good," he said in a low voice. "Lots better than Selene."

"Selene's fine now," I told him. "Miss Perkins was right about the spell. She said it would break when the sun came up, and it did. Just like that—Erica knew who she was, and so did Selene."

"Must've been mighty bad news for that poor girl—her parents being dead and all. Ain't no fun losing your mom, I can tell you that, brother."

"She's going to be all right. The O'Neills treat her like a granddaughter."

While we had a glass of milk and some cookies, I told Brody what he wanted to hear—all the details of Erica's rescue.

When I was done, Brody said, "I been telling the kids at school about you going to the cabin and seeing Old Auntie and her hog. Boy, was they surprised you done that. Didn't think you had the guts."

Brody helped himself to more cookies and grinned at me. "When I tell them what you done to get your sister back, they'll all want to be your friend."

I took a handful of cookies and grinned back at him. "You want to climb Brewster's Hill and take a look at what's left of the cabin?"

Brody swallowed a mouthful of cookies and thought about it. "You sure Old Auntie's really gone, both her and that hog?"

"I told you, Bloody Bones fell off the cliff and broke into bits, and Old Auntie died in the fire."

Brody dipped his last cookie into his milk and shrugged. "You mind if I whistle for Bella? She's good company."

So with Bella leading the way, Brody and I climbed the trail to the top of Brewster's Hill. The dog acted as if there was nothing to fear in the hollow. In fact, she ran over and peed on the charred wood just as if she were saying it was her place now.

While Bella sniffed in the ruins, Brody and I kicked at the logs and poked around in the ashes as if we were looking for something. I don't know what. Just something.

Brody wandered over to the chimney, which was still standing. "Daniel!" he yelled. "Come here!"

He was backing away from whatever it was, plainly scared. I ran to see what he'd found. Little Erica lay in the ashes, looking up at me with one eye, almost as if she were winking. The other eye had melted into its socket. Her hair was singed, and her face was black and wrinkled from the fire, but it was Little Erica all right.

Looking at the doll made me feel as if I were about to throw up the cookies I'd stuffed myself with before we'd left the house.

"It's my sister's doll," I told him.

"The one that started all the trouble?" He looked puzzled. "But she's little, like a plain old ordinary kid's doll. You told me she growed big and come to life."

"When the spell broke, I guess she changed back to what she really was—a lump of plastic, mostly melted now."

"You ain't going to give her back to your sister, are you?"

"Erica doesn't want anything to do with dolls anymore."

I couldn't take my eyes away from Little Erica.

She had a wicked look, like some kind of shrunken mummy—maybe because of the fire, maybe because of something else.

Bella ambled over to see what we were looking at. As soon as she saw the doll, she whined and backed away. She was shivering the way she had the night we'd visited the cabin and seen Old Auntie and Bloody Bones.

"You think it's okay to leave her here?" Brody asked. He was worried about the doll, too. I could tell by his voice.

I shook my head. Little Erica didn't seem like a lump of plastic anymore, and I didn't want someone to find her. What if a bit of Old Auntie was in that doll?

"Let's bury her," Brody said.

Using boards from the cabin, the two of us dug a hole by the fireplace, making it as deep as we could. The ground there was soft despite the cold, probably because of the fire.

Neither of us wanted to touch the doll, so we scooped her out of the ashes with one of the boards we used to dig with. We dumped dirt on her, stamping it down with our feet so it was as hard as we could make it. Then we pulled and tugged and pushed stones from the old wall and piled them on top of the grave.

"There," Brody said. "She won't never get out now."

Wiping our hands on our jeans, we whistled for Bella and hiked down the trail toward home.

Summer, Two Years Later

An old woman stands on the hilltop, just on the edge of the green woods, smiling down on the farmhouse below. What she sees pleases her. The house has a new roof and a fresh coat of pale blue paint. The junk in the yard is gone. The barn has been cleaned out and repaired. The woman who lives in the house uses it for a workroom. She's in there now, weaving a rug on a loom. The old woman hears the music she plays – folk songs, ballads, with fiddles and dulcimers, tunes she's known all her life.

A man mows the grass in the front yard. He's riding one of those little tractor things they use now. Flowers bloom along a picket fence – daisies, black-eyed Susans, coneflowers, bright colors, bees swarming. A vegetable garden behind the house grows strong and healthy, just as it ought to. They'll have tomatoes, squash, beans, lettuce, spinach, even some corn. More than they can eat, but they've built a stand at the end of the driveway where they sell the extra.

The old woman watches Daniel play catch with Brody, the boy who lives down the road. She watches Erica and Selene take turns swinging on a tire hung from a high branch. She hears them laugh, all four of them.

She sees the woman come out of the barn and cross the yard, shooing chickens out of her way. A few minutes later she calls the children to come into the house and cool off with lemonade.

"Well, Auntie," the old woman says to someone she can't see, someone who once roamed these woods and watched the farmhouse with dark intent. "You been took yourself, and I aim to make sure you stay took. These children don't recollect a thing about you, except sometimes when they dream. But we all got nightmares, don't we? Then morning comes and sweeps them away like cobwebs."

Walking slowly and carefully, the old woman climbs the trail to the top of Brewster's Hill. Vines and weeds have grown over the charred wood. Wildflowers sway in the breeze. A mockingbird sings in a nearby tree.

With her walking staff, the old woman pokes at the ashes, as if she's making sure the fire's out and Auntie and Bloody Bones are still took. She pays close attention to the stones piled up near what's left of the chimney. A tall clump of Queen Anne's lace almost hides the burial place. All is as it should be. Calm. Peaceful.

The old woman sits down on the stone wall to rest. She watches a butterfly flit among the flowers. Bees hum in the wild clover.

One of her cats has followed her, solid black except for a little white spot on its chest.

"Cat, come set a spell." She pats her lap, and the cat curls up on the old woman's bony knees.

"You and me and that boy, we done good work that snowy night." She strokes the cat until its whole body vibrates with a rumbly purr. "We made us our own tale, didn't we—a tale like the tellers told back and back and back to the first tellers sitting around their fires, keeping the dark away with their words."

The old woman yawns. Before she stands up, the cat jumps off her lap and the two of them disappear into the green woods.